Blue Lightning

Carnival of Mysteries Season 2

BL Maxwell

COPYRIGHT

BLUE LIGHTNING

CARNIVAL OF MYSTERIES 2

This book may not be reproduced, scanned, or distributed in any printed or electronic form without permissions from the author, except for using small quotes for book review quotations. All characters and storylines are the property of the author. The characters, events and places portrayed in this book are fictitious. Any similarity to real persons, living or dead, is coincidentaland not intended by the author.

Trademarks:

This book identifies product names and services known to be trademarks, registered trademarks, or service marks of their respective holders. The author acknowledges the trademarked status and trademark owners of all products referenced in this work of fiction. The publication and use of these trademarks is not authorized, associated with, or sponsored by the trademark owners.

Warning:

Intended for a mature 18+ audience only. This book contains material that may be offensive to some and is intended for a mature, adult audience. It contains graphic language, explicit sexual content, and adult situations.

ONE

Cole Ryan

NOTHING EVER HAPPENS IN this town. The words were on repeat in my mind as my feet pounded the pavement of the country road I was currently jogging on. I'd lived in Hickory Crossing for all of my thirty years, and not once had something happened that surprised me or was unusual. It was always chronically the same as it was yesterday. It was my own damn fault. I'd been offered a scholarship from one of the state colleges to run track for them after high school, but that all sounded so scary when I was a teenager who had never gone past the county line.

Now I was just stupid enough to stay here and let life pass me by as I complained daily about how boring my life was.

"Mornin', Cole," Miss Avery said, as I ran past her small farm like I did pretty much every morning. She lived alone and ran her small goat farm by herself. I waved to her and continued on my way, grumbling under my breath about how every damn morning it was the same old thing.

The sun was barely rising as I crossed the four-way stop and ran on toward town. It had rained nearly every day the past week, and it was nice to have one morning where I wasn't soaked to the bone by the time I got back to my house. I needed to run, and rain or not, I was still going to go. The clouds rolled in heavy and within a few minutes it looked like rain was a given. "Fuck," I said under my breath and picked up the pace.

A rumble in the distance told me it wasn't going to be long before once again I was getting rained on. I glanced back at the gathering storm and noticed something I'd never seen before. The clouds were dark, but they seemed to glow an electric blue. I stopped running and cupped my hands over my eyes, squinting and straining to get a better look and some understanding of exactly what I was looking at. It was strange, and I wondered if maybe the sun was illuminating the clouds from behind but that didn't explain the blue color. "The sun is behind me," I mumbled, still not sure what I was seeing.

Electricity crackled in the air as the first flash of lightning brightened the sky just before a loud crack of thunder startled me. I turned again and started running, and hoped I could get home before it all hit. The sound of my shoes on the pavement was amplified, and the hairs on my legs and arms stood on end. Ozone was thick and heavy in the air, and I knew it was only a matter of time before it hit.

Three things happened at once. There was a flash of blue that I knew was lightning. A clap of thunder hit so loud and hard I felt the ground shake under my feet just before I was launched through the air and landed in the grass at the side of the road. My breath was knocked out of me, and the thought crossed my mind I could be hurt really badly. Then there was nothing.

"Hey, buddy, are you okay?"

I struggled to open my eyes, but it was pouring rain and my whole body ached. I sucked in a deep breath and coughed out a lungful of smoke. *What the*—Forcing my eyes open, the first thing I saw was a head full of light blond hair and bright green eyes filled with worry. "Are ye okay?" he asked in a slight accent I knew I should recognize but my brain was still stuck on the fact I'd exhaled a bunch of smoke.

"What happened?" I finally managed to croak out.

"I think you got hit by lightning," he said, and helped me to a sitting position.

"What?"

"I said I think—"

"I heard what you said, but that can't be right. I was just running and then—" I couldn't remember what happened next.

"You don't remember?" he asked.

"I guess not," I said, and wondered where my shoes were because I knew for a fact, I'd had them on earlier. I glanced around and after he helped me stand, I slowly walked over to where I was when I'd been running. There, in the middle of the road, were two burn marks that looked suspiciously the same size as my footprints. "Where are my shoes?"

"Let me take a look. I was wondering why you were out here barefooted." He walked back over to the side of the road while I stared at the burnt impressions that definitely looked like footprints. "Is this one of them?" He walked closer to me holding a scrap of the white leather that had once been an expensive pair of running shoes.

"I think so, I mean maybe?" If I didn't know that was a part of my shoe, I wouldn't have recognized it. It was charred black and what wasn't burnt, was melted. I looked down at my feet, and the band that was at the top of my socks was still there, but that was it. That was all that remained of my shoes and my socks.

"How do you suppose that happened?" the guy asked, and I realized he was standing next to me staring at my burnt shoe impressions with me.

"I think you're right. I got struck by lightning."

"What do you remember?" he asked and stood with his hands on his hips waiting for me to answer as though he were talking about a vacation I'd taken or possibly a long lost memory.

"Nothing. I was out for a run and the next thing I remember is you waking me up." As soon as the words were out of my mouth, I found it harder to believe that's what had happened, but there was no other explanation.

"Are you sure you're not hurt?" he asked and gave me a onceover.

I patted the pockets of my running shorts and my light jacket. Nothing hurt anywhere, but on closer inspection the zipper to my jacket was fused and burn marks were visible at the bottom. "I don't think it got me."

"Oh, it definitely got you," he mumbled. "Come on then, I'll give you a ride home." He led me to the small van he was driving while I tried to comprehend what was happening.

"I don't think I should get in the car with you. I mean I don't know who you are." That was the first thing my parents taught me when I was a kid: don't get into a car with a stranger. And right now, that simple lesson was kicking in strong.

"I promise I'm not a bad guy. I'm making a delivery for a paper company. A place in town ordered some of our finest linen paper for a project. The boss wanted me to deliver it in person, so they get to know us a little better. He's all about the personal touch. The name's Bobby Sanders." He held his hand out to me, and I stared at it for a full minute before my brain kicked in and I shook it.

"I'm Cole Ryan." Thunder rumbled in the distance and once again the clouds threatened to rain down on us.

"Well, Cole Ryan, unless you don't mind walking back to town in your bare feet during a rainstorm, I'd love to offer you a ride." He grinned, and all I sensed from him was his want to help me.

I thought about it, and tried to gauge how fit he was and if I'd be able to wrestle away from him if he tried to hold me captive, before realizing he was still waiting for my answer. Hickory Crossing was about five miles away and while I didn't want to risk my safety, I wasn't sure I could walk it. "Sure, I'll take a ride. But if you try anything just know I will fight you for everything." I pointed my finger at him to punctuate my words, and he responded by holding his hands up in defeat.

"I promise I won't try anything. Just doing my good deed for the day," he said, before turning to walk to his van.

I followed behind him and noticed it was still running. He opened his door, and I took a deep breath before opening the passenger door and sliding into the seat.

"So, what do you do in Hickory Crossing, Cole Ryan?" he asked as he put the van in gear and drove toward town.

"Apparently run in rainstorms and get struck by lightning," I muttered, making him laugh while I once again questioned my sanity.

"Well, hopefully you don't do that too often," he said, and reached across to turn on the radio.

Two

Bobby Sanders

I GLANCED AT THE guy sitting in the seat of the work van. His hair was jet black and stood up all over his head. The ends of it looked like they'd been burnt off and soot or ash was smeared on his face. He appeared confused, and I didn't want to worry him, but I'd seen what had happened and was amazed he'd survived.

I'd noticed him in the distance as I approached the small town my dad had sent me to. It was in the middle of nowhere and hidden in the heavy growth of oak trees, all of which looked ancient. The sky had grown dark, and in the distance, I would have sworn the clouds were illuminated with a strange blue glow just before a loud clap of thunder sounded at the same time a bolt of lightning hit him and blew him onto the side of the road.

I slammed on the brakes with both feet and ran to where I'd seen him land. There he was in a smoking heap, shoeless and not breathing. I thought he was dead until he sucked in a breath and blew out a puff of smoke. I was so shocked that for a moment I couldn't react, but I tried to stay calm because there was no way he could know how lucky he was.

His shoes had all but melted off him, and his jacket and shorts didn't fare much better. His eyes were wide in fright or shock, I wasn't sure which. I had to help him, and I couldn't just leave him out there on his own. So when he hesitated to get in the van, I did all I could to reassure him, and as he sat next to me now, I was glad I hadn't just left him there. His hands shook as they rested on his legs, and he rocked forward in his seat. He needed more help than I could give him.

"Is there a hospital nearby?" I asked and knew what his answer would be.

"The nearest one is twenty minutes away. Why?" he asked and met my eyes. His eyes were filled with terror which was more than easy to understand. He had to be in shock to not realize he needed to see a doctor.

"Don't worry, I'll get you there." I hit the gas and drove as fast as I could while he gave me directions. "At least the rain let up." As soon as the words were out of my mouth the skies opened up, and it was raining so hard I was forced to slow down for fear of driving off the road or hitting a slow-moving car ahead of me. His groan had me trying to push it and drive faster, but there wasn't a chance of going any faster without getting us both killed.

"It's okay. I'm sorry. I'm just—" His words were cut off as his back arched and he started to convulse.

"Fuck!" I yelled before cranking the wheel and slamming on the brakes. "Hey. Hey, look at me," I said while tapping his cheek. "Come on, man. I told you I'd drive you to the hospital, but I have no clue what to do." He stopped seizing, but his eyes were still rolled back, and he was frozen in the same position. His head thrown back against the headrest, his back arched, and his hands both clenched into claws. "Come on, Cole, it's going to be okay, I promise."

Suddenly he sucked in a deep shuddering breath and slowly relaxed back into the seat. "I—I'm okay."

"No, you're not, you just had a seizure." I brushed the hair back from his face and felt the texture of sooty ash that I refused to think about too much, but imagined it was probably burnt skin cells. "We'll be at the hospital within twenty minutes. Try to relax and I'll hurry." My own body started to shake, and I forced myself to stay in control and be calm, but I was so ill-equipped to deal with someone who had just been struck by lightning. "I probably should have called an ambulance," I rambled.

"Water," he said. His voice was dry and brittle sounding.

"Sure," I said and scrambled to find something besides the coffee I had in the center console. Finally, after reaching behind both seats and digging around underneath them, I found a half-full bottle of water. "Here, sorry it's already open."

Without a second thought he took it from me and drank it all down. "Thank you," he said, and glanced at me. He looked better, not so pale and definitely more relaxed. Then I realized I was staring at him. His eyes were beautiful, and in the back of my mind I thought it was strange I'd notice that in the middle of a crisis. And by crisis I meant the guy had just been struck by lightning and likely had internal injuries or possibly his brain had been partially fried. I shook my head and looked away from him to get my focus back on the task at hand, getting him some help.

Checking it was clear to pull out, I merged back onto the highway, and drove as fast as I could in the shitty conditions. Twenty minutes later to the second, we were pulling into the hospital parking lot. Driving right up to the emergency room entrance, I was relieved there were no other cars parked there. It was a smaller hospital, but you never knew what you were going to run into. Considering all the farms in the area I imagined they treated their share of accidents related to machinery or livestock. Hopefully someone would know how to help Cole.

"You can just leave me," Coal said from the passenger seat, still slumped over with his eyes closed.

"No, I don't think I'll be doing that. Wait right here. I'll go get someone." Before he could protest, I got out of the van and ran to the door. "Help. I brought someone in who was struck by lightning," I said to no one in particular and hoped the right person would hear.

"Where are we going?" a female orderly asked as she hurried to me pushing a wheelchair.

"This way." She followed me to the van and the two of us helped ease Cole into the chair.

"You'll need to give the front desk your information," she said before hurrying him off to the back.

"Fill this out." A clipboard was shoved at me, and when I turned away from the desk, it was to a waiting room packed with other patients. I took the last open seat between a mum and little boy who was clutching a bucket, and an older man with a large bloody bandage on his hand.

"Did your friend really get struck by lightning?" the older man on my right asked.

"Yeah. Blue lightning to be specific." I looked at the paper attached to the clipboard, but all the information they wanted was on Cole and I had zero clue how to fill it out since I didn't know him at all. I stood to walk back to the desk when the man grabbed my arm. I looked from him to his hand, but he still didn't pull it back.

"You say blue lightning?" he asked as he squinted his eyes and seemed to brace for my reply.

Tucking the clipboard under my arm I peeled his fingers loose, but he didn't react at all as his eyes were still trained on me waiting for me to answer. "Yeah. He was jogging and the storm moved in fast on him. He didn't have a chance to get under cover, I guess. I'm not really sure. I was driving past and just happened to see it happen." I realized I'd started to ramble and promptly clamped my mouth shut.

"With a flash of blue," he mumbled but then turned away and mumbled more to himself. I hurried over to the reception desk, and hoped they didn't need more information than his name and what I'd seen happen to him because that was all I had.

THREE

Cole

"HE'S NOT CONSCIOUS, WE need to start him on fluids. He has second-degree burns on the bottoms of both feet and his left hand," someone said from my side. I tried to open my eyes but couldn't. It was as though all the energy I normally had was drained from me. I could hear all they said around me, but I was hopeless to respond in any way.

My eye barely opened when one of them lifted the eyelid. "Sir, can you tell us what happened?" a man about my age asked as he tapped my cheek, and I struggled to crack open my eyes.

"Lightning," I managed to say.

"You were struck by lightning?" he asked.

I could only nod in reply as my eyes slid shut again.

"Sir, I need you to stay awake. We want to make sure you're not hurt more badly than it appears," he explained, but I knew exactly how bad it looked.

"Did you say someone brought him in?" the male voice asked.

"Yes, he's out front," someone standing right next to me said.

"Go get him. I need to ask him a few questions."

There was silence then beyond the sounds of metal clanking together and shoes on the hard floor. I drifted, and for a time forgot where I was as emotions passed over me that reminded me of when I was a small child and had been injured. The caring way my mother had looked after any injuries made me forget I'd been hurt at all. In the end all that was left were feelings of peace, warmth, and love.

"I don't really know how I can help," a familiar voice said as it drew nearer.

"What did you see," the voice from earlier asked.

"He was jogging, and the weather got ugly really fast. He was struck by a bolt of lightning that blew him about ten feet over to the side of the road. When I got to him, he was smoldering. His shoes were blown off, he was unconscious, and covered in soot or ash."

"When he came to, what was his state of mind?" A light was shone in my eyes and a needle was jabbed in my hand as I tried not to wince.

"He was lucid, told me his name, and fought me about having me give him a ride."

"What do you mean?" the voice, who must have been the doctor, asked.

"I think he was afraid I was going to abduct him, but I only wanted to get him some help. He was aware of what was going on, but there was no way he would have been able to walk back to town. We were about twenty minutes from here when he had a seizure."

"How do you know it was a seizure," another voice asked, making me wonder how many people were in the room, but I was still too weak to open my eyes.

"One minute he was sitting in the car seat covered in ash, burnt hair, and no shoes, and talking to me. The next minute his eyes rolled back in his head, and his back arched off the seat while he shook. Does that sound like a seizure to you?" Bobby asked. Bobby. I was surprised I remembered his name, but his voice was familiar to me. It was the first thing I remembered from after I'd been knocked out. For a moment everyone was quiet before one of them started barking out orders.

"I want a full panel of tests, let's figure out what we're actually dealing with," the same voice who had questioned Bobby now said. The room was a jumble of motion and sounds as everyone was either poking or prodding at me in various ways. Then a wave of calm washed over me. *You'll be okay*, I heard someone say, or maybe I imagined it. A strong hand took mine and squeezed it tight.

"Don't worry, Cole, I'm not leaving until I know you're being properly taken care of," Bobby said from my side.

I wanted to thank him, or at least open my eyes, but all I could manage was to cling to his hand for all it was worth. And right now, it was worth a lot. My mind drifted, and I was in that strange state between wakefulness and sleep where you're completely aware of everything around you, but it takes on a dream state. Occasionally strange thoughts crossed my mind that I knew were not my own. Some were focused on medical care, while others were random feelings of worry for someone I couldn't picture.

Flashes of images crossed my mind, none of them were visible long enough for me to interpret what they were, and before I could think about it too much, I fell asleep and dreamed. This dream was different than any other before. I don't know how I knew but I did. It started with me running down the road I'd run on nearly every day for as long as I could remember. The sound of my shoes on the pavement sounded the same, and I thought in the dream I'd at least get to finish my run. Of course I wasn't that lucky. Dark clouds rolled in fast, and out of the corner of my eye I saw a faint blue glow in the clouds. When I turned my head to get a better look it wasn't visible. My eyes were drawn to my hands that now glowed the same blue I'd seen hidden in the rolling clouds.

"What the—" I started to ask but all my thoughts and words were cut off when a slicing pain cut through my skull. My subconscious was ripped from my body, and I was floating above the gurney I lay on. Bobby knelt next to the hospital bed, still holding my hand while everyone else in the room rushed around me. Time stood still until slowly, Bobby looked up, and I would have sworn his eyes met mine.

Four

Bobby

"Sir, you need to move aside," one of the medical professionals said, and I started to release his hand. But then something drew my attention to the ceiling in the room where they were now feverishly working on Cole. In a matter of seconds, he'd gone from in and out of consciousness to no heartbeat, and if I had to guess he looked dead. I didn't know this guy. I hadn't met him at all until a few short minutes ago, but right now something told me if I let go of his hand, he'd never see the light of day again.

"I'm not moving," I said before I could even think about the consequences of it and tried to stay out of their way as they hurried around him trying to save his life. One of them started chest compressions while another used a mask with a ball pump to force oxygen into his lungs. His skin was grey and his whole body was limp. The hand I clung to was lifeless, and when I glanced at his face, his eyes were half open and staring blankly at nothing. "Come on, Cole, fight." Squeezing his hand far too tight, I hoped it didn't hurt him while at the same time I hoped it got his attention.

A rumble sounded in the distance, but I barely heard it over the noise of the medical staff trying to save Cole's life.

"Stop compressions," the doctor said, and everyone stood back while he listened for a heartbeat, but he shook his head and stood back for the nurses to go back to trying to get his heart beating.

"Doctor—" One of the nurses paused and waited to see what happened next.

"Get the crash cart," he said, and a nurse rushed over to Cole wheeling a cart that had brought into the room a few seconds earlier. He picked up the two handles and held them out while a nurse applied gel. "Everyone, stand back."

His eyes met mine and I knew he meant me, but I just couldn't make myself let go. I closed my eyes and prepared for what could very well be the shock of my life. The building rumbled and shook with a roll of thunder and I clenched his hand tighter.

"What the fuck is that?" someone said just before the building started to rattle and the machine sounded an alarm that it was charged. Bottles and instruments started to fall off tables and shelves and the whole room was in motion. The bed moved with the vibration, and a few people tried to cover their heads while others tried to cover Cole.

The air around us changed, and my ears popped as the vibration turned to a deep hum that pulsed against my chest. My eyes were all over the place, not knowing where to look or what I should do, when suddenly Cole gripped my hand. Not the gentle squeeze of someone who had just come back to life, but the grip of someone with far more strength than me.

His body crackled with electricity as sparks flickered and danced across his body. The hair on my arms stood up and

I really hoped I wasn't about to get shocked by whatever the fuck was going on. But then I realized the electricity was only on Cole. None of it touched me where I held his hand, almost as though it avoided my skin and anyone else who was nearby.

Slowly his body started to levitate off the bed. There were shouts of shock and disbelief but all I could focus on was Cole and how tight he still gripped my hand. Lightning crackled and wrapped around him.

"With a flash of blue there will be two. One of old, and one of new. Wisdom and innocence must combine, if one of them is to remain alive," Cole said, but it wasn't his voice. It boomed with power that shook the walls of the room even more than the thunder or whatever had shaken it a few seconds before. I stood and braced myself against the bed to stop from being thrown all over the room. His hand was still clenched in mine, but I looked at his face while the voice spoke. His lips didn't move, and he still looked grey.

Whisps of blue electric bolts wrapped around his arms, legs, and body as he continued to rise higher off the bed. The noise in the room rose to a deafening roar and I wondered if a tornado had hit and we were in the middle of it, before I remembered we were nowhere near where a tornado would or could form.

With a whoosh, everything stopped, and the room fell silent as Cole flopped down on the bed at the same time the noise ended. As soon as his body hit the bed he sucked in a big breath of air and his eyes opened. "What happened?" he said and looked around in a panic.

"Sir, you had a—I'm not sure what happened, but you've had an incident," the doctor said.

"Bobby, get me out of here," he said. His eyes were wide with fright, and his grip on my hand tightened even more while he grabbed at wires and anything else that was attached to him with the other hand.

"Sir, please calm down. It's a really bad idea for you to leave," one of the nurses pleaded.

"Bobby, I can't stay here." His eyes begged me to understand, and help, and a voice in the back of my head told me to get him the hell out. Something took over and I had to restrain myself from shoving everyone away from him.

"He can leave if he wants to." I helped him stand and draped a hospital gown around him when it was obvious there wasn't enough of his shirt and shorts left to worry about. He clung to my arm as a nurse brought a wheelchair for him to sit in.

"Are you sure you want to leave?" he asked as he helped me ease Cole into the chair.

"I'm sure," Cole said.

"You'll need to sign this." A woman in scrubs brought a clipboard to Cole and held it for him while he struggled to grip the pen enough to sign it.

"Thank you, I'm sorry," Cole said before reaching back to squeeze my hand where I gripped the handles of the wheelchair.

As soon as he'd finished, I hurried through the door and back out to the van that was still where I'd left it near the emergency room door. "Are you sure you're okay to leave?" I asked him as I helped him into the seat.

"No, but if I stay there everyone else is in danger." His eyes met mine and the electric blue color seemed to glow, mesmerizing me. "Including you."

I glanced away and forced myself to consider how deeply I wanted to get into things with this guy that I didn't even know. But a force I couldn't deny—or resist—pulled me to him. "Let's get you something to eat, and maybe some clothes."

He looked down at the hospital gown he now wore and at his feet where the tops of his socks were all that remained. "And some shoes," he said, before meeting my eyes with a grin.

That grin did something to me that I wasn't willing to name, and I forced myself to give him some distance as I helped him buckle his seat belt. But when I met his eyes again, he was still grinning. I looked away and chuckled. "And some shoes."

FIVE

Cole

A flash of blue, a flash of blue, a flash of blue, a flash of blue. Over and over the words repeated in my mind. But the voice saying them wasn't my own, and the ripple of energy that pulsed under my skin wasn't something I'd experienced before either. The lightning was just there, and I knew if I reached for it—

"What did you want to eat?" Bobby asked, and I turned to look at him.

"A burger and onion rings, maybe a chocolate shake." As soon as he mentioned food my stomach growled. I'd eaten breakfast like I always did, a protein shake and a granola bar, but I wasn't sure how long ago that had been.

"Do you want to go buy some clothes?" he asked, and I wondered how he was staying so calm about this weird situation he'd been thrown into.

"Let's get some food and then if you don't mind just taking me home, I'd appreciate it." I mean I had clothes at home, and at this point it didn't matter if I was riding around in just a hospital gown. "Then I can pay you back too. I don't want you to think I expect you to feed me after driving me all the way to the hospital."

"What happened back there?" He asked the one thing I hadn't wanted to even think about as he pulled off the highway and into a Sonic. After finding a parking space under the awning and near one of the menus, I could feel his eyes on me as he waited for me to reply.

My stomach growled, and I was focused on the menu and if I wanted one burger or possibly two when he squeezed my arm getting my attention. "Sorry, I guess I really am hungrier than I thought I was. I don't know what it was. There were so many things happening all at once."

"Do you remember it all?" he asked and stared at me. I turned to face him and once again was struck with how easy he was to be with.

I considered lying to him. I knew they all thought I was so out of it I wouldn't remember what had happened. "I remember," I whispered.

"Everything?" he asked.

"Can I take your order?" a voice through the intercom squawked, making us both jump.

"Yeah," I said, and proceeded to order way too much food for one person before asking Bobby what he wanted.

"I'll have a cheeseburger and tater tots," he said.

"Something to drink?" the intercom voice asked.

After ordering lemonade the two of us sat in silence while we waited for our food to be delivered. I thought about ignoring his question and playing dumb, but he'd helped me when he didn't have to. I owed him an explanation. "I don't know what happened. I've never had anything close to what happened earlier happen to me."

"Do you think it's from being struck by lightning?" he asked, and I noticed his accent again.

"Are you Irish?"

"Yeah, I've been here a few years now. My dad is from the US, Sugarfield to be exact, and my ma is from Dublin. I grew up there."

"What made you decide to move here?"

"They owned a print shop in Dublin and wanted to open a branch here. I thought they were crazy when they first came up with the idea, but my sister is running the place in Dublin, and it's all worked out so far. We go back a time or two a year." The faraway look in his eyes told me he missed his homeland, and I wondered once again why he'd leave there to move to Sugarfield.

"I don't think I've been to Sugarfield before," I said and hoped it kept the conversation off what had happened.

"You didn't miss much," he said with a chuckle. "It's not more than a wide spot in the road, but we really only need the space for the printing machines and paper storage. So, for us it works out great."

"Oh god, did I screw up your work schedule?" It hit me that he was at work, or driving to work, when he found me. I hadn't taken any consideration to the fact that this wasn't part of his plan for the day.

"Nope, I called Dad, and he completely understood and wants an update on the poor guy who got hit by lightning." He smiled at me then, and something in that smile made me feel a little better. Even if I was sitting here at a Sonic waiting for food in a hospital gown.

I glanced at myself in the rear-view mirror and couldn't believe my eyes. "Oh my god." I tried to smooth my hair down, but my hand was covered in ash from just touching it. I still had soot or ash or whatever all over my body except where the hospital had wiped it off to either stick something to my skin, or to draw blood.

"Yeah, that's gonna take a minute to grow back," Bobby said, like he was reassuring me the haircut I got wasn't so bad.

"It's all burnt," I said, and forced myself not to touch it any more than I had to. Then I noticed the red spots on my hand where it had been burned. Now it looked nearly healed. I covered it with my other hand and squirmed in my seat.

A flash of blue.

I ignored the words that continued to float through my mind since we'd left the hospital. It had to be from the lightning. I mean everything was from the lightning. Maybe it just zapped my brain in some way. *Just* zapped my brain. Like that could be a good thing in any way.

"Here you go," a server wearing skates said as she rolled up to the window and settled the tray of food there. I was happy for the mental distraction, because so far, every time I thought about it, the voice in my head was there and I forced myself not to worry if it was truly from the lightning or if I was losing my fucking mind. Because that voice was definitely not mine.

Six

Bobby

COLE PASSED ME THE food I'd ordered and the two of us settled in to eat while watching everyone else either order their food or eat in their cars like we were. I'd lied when I said my dad was okay with me taking him to the hospital. He was worried, but he was also concerned we'd lose the new contract with the small company in Hickory Crossing.

"What do you do in Hickory Crossing?" I asked. This whole situation was strange. We hadn't really talked at all on the way to the hospital since he was injured so badly, and then after what happened while he was there . . . I decided I needed to not think about it for now. There would be time for us to figure it out later. Maybe.

"I work at the sporting goods store."

"Do your parents own it?" I asked. Since moving here, I'd found out most businesses in the small towns that surrounded Sugarfield were family owned.

"No, but a family friend does." He took a big bite of his burger and groaned. He'd been through it that's for sure, but I couldn't lay to rest the feeling that he still wasn't okay. There was a strange energy I could feel from him that felt a lot like a warning. "I started working there in high school, and now I manage it. It's okay I suppose, I mean it could be worse." It seemed there was a story there, but if he wasn't willing to offer more information, I wasn't going to keep pushing.

"That is true. I once worked for a cleanout company that cleared out apartments after someone moved out. You would not believe the shit people leave behind." I wasn't sure why I told him that. I hadn't thought about that job in years. It had been an attempt to go get my own job and not be so dependent on my family business for work. But after a few weeks I realized the printing business was much better than sorting through belongings that were both sad and disgusting.

"How was that?" he asked and stopped midchew to listen.

"Horrible," I said, and we both laughed.

"I can't even imagine." He took another big bite of burger and we both went back to people watching.

"Did you want anything else?" I asked after the two of us had finished eating, which took less than ten minutes.

"Nope, I'm good." If he wasn't dressed like an escapee from a hospital and still looking like he'd been blown up, I would have thought we were just out for the day. I couldn't understand how he could seem so unaffected by it all.

"Let's get you back home then," I said, and after the server came out to take our tray away, we were back on the road. It was a short twenty-minute drive back to Hickory Crossing. I took the tree-lined backroads and stayed off the busy freeway. It was still overcast but the sky wasn't as angry as it had been earlier.

"When you were out, there was a strange noise and wind that ripped through the hospital. I would have sworn it was a tornado," I said and hoped he didn't just shut me down.

"We don't get tornadoes here," he said.

"I thought the same thing."

"I heard it. The humming, and the wind. Everything flying around in the room before the electricity was coursing through my body."

"I could see it moving over your skin. There were pulses of energy, but I couldn't feel it. It should have electrocuted me, but it didn't," I said. That was one of the stranger parts of the whole experience. How it seemed to encase him in the blue electric glow of the surge of power, but none of it touched or harmed me. "The hair on my arms stood up, but there was no pain."

"Was it stranger than me levitating off the bed?" Cole asked and shot me a look. I wasn't sure if he was testing me to see if I really was okay with everything I'd seen or if he needed to say it out loud to himself.

"I didn't think you remembered that. I've never seen anything like that in my life. Or heard of it either. That only happens in movies or in magic acts."

"That's what I thought before today, but now I don't know. Everything was strange about that storm. It moved in really fast, and I would have sworn I saw the clouds glowing blue just before I was struck."

"I saw that too, and the lightning that hit you glowed blue."

"But what does it mean?" he asked.

"I have no clue. But if you want me to, I'll help you find out," I said before I had time to think about what I was offering. I had zero clue about any of this stuff, but I meant what I said, I'd help him.

"I think I need help," he admitted, and his head slumped forward. "It was probably stupid to leave the hospital, but they can't help me with this."

"While I understand you wanting to leave, and honestly I think the hospital was relieved to see you go, I do think you need to have a doctor check you over to make sure there's nothing wrong."

"You're probably right. My parents are going to lose their shit," he said, and for a moment looked like a teenager bracing for a scolding.

"There is no good way to say you were hit by lightning. I'd be surprised if one of the people that live out there didn't see it. It looked like an electrical explosion from where I was."

"I don't remember that part. I was jogging and then it started to rain really hard. The next thing I remember is you standing there. But I don't know how I got there, and I didn't have any pain. Which is surprising since it melted my shoes and socks off. How can that happen?" he asked.

"I'm not sure. But I am glad you weren't hurt any worse. I watched a show about people who'd been struck by lightning. If it goes through your body, it usually blows apart the area it comes out of. You got very lucky." I had shoved that information into the back of my mind but what happened to him was not like what I'd seen happen to any of the people on the show.

"Me too, but it feels like I should have been."

"Let's just focus on the fact that you weren't, and we'll try to figure out why the lightning was blue. How does that sound?" The more we talked about it, the stranger I knew it was. But none of this was normal, and I still had no clue how I was really going to help him other than to be there and assure him that it really had happened. I thought about the strange pulse of power that danced so close to my skin I could feel it like a caress. My eyes threatened to close at the sensation, then I realized I wasn't just imagining it, it was true.

SEVEN

Cole

I LISTENED AS HE described what he'd seen but then I felt a pull as he spoke, and it wasn't me leaning out to touch him. It was the strange power that had somehow found its way under my skin. A crackle of blue reached out to his arm and played along his skin, and I could feel it as though I were touching him myself.

His gasp caught my attention as he pulled over to the side of the road. "Are you hurt?" I asked, because I wasn't sure what the hell was happening.

"I can feel you," he all but shouted. His eyes were wide with equal parts of shock and wonder. "How can this be?" His voice was filled with wonder and excitement.

"I can feel you too," I admitted. "I can feel your skin as though I'm touching you."

"How can this be?" he repeated.

I extended my finger to the spark of electricity that played along my hand. It wasn't painful and strangely enough it felt like it was just a part of me. *With a flash of blue.*

"What did you say?" he asked.

"Nothing, what did you hear?" I'd been hearing those words on repeat since we'd left the hospital. Ignoring it didn't make it go away, but it helped me to not focus on it so much.

"With a flash of blue. That's what I heard."

"That's impossible." I wasn't going to go down that path. None of this made sense and all of it was fucking weird. But I wasn't willing to even imagine that he could read my thoughts. Or maybe I was showing him my thoughts? I didn't know how that worked, or if it was even possible.

"You know what that means?" he asked and turned to face me.

I hadn't wanted to tell him. Hell, I didn't want to admit it to myself, but I remembered every word of the strange poem I'd heard while I was levitating above the bed. "No, but I remember it."

"You said that when you were levitating above the bed. But your voice wasn't your own. It was infused with so much power, and you clenched my hand the whole time with a strength that didn't seem possible. Whose voice was that?" he asked and reached across the console for my hand.

"I've never heard those words until today, and I don't know how I knew it. Those words were not my own, I don't understand it, but somehow, I know someone else was speaking through me." That was it, that was what a part of me screamed. Someone else could read my thoughts and was able to speak through me without me being able to stop them.

"Is that possible?" he asked and furrowed his brow.

The laugh that came out of me sounded like a crazed person, but right now I was on the edge of either losing my mind or gaining some clarity about shit I had no clue even existed. "You saw me get hit by lightning and levitate off a bed. You think psychic abilities are over the top after all that?" I smiled, and it felt so fucking good but slightly foreign to feel that sense of relief.

He squeezed my hand, and I was struck by how normal it felt for this stranger to hold my hand. "You're right, at this point nothing should shock me. There's a strange feeling I get when we're close. It's like nothing I've ever experienced. It's not just attraction, it's—well I don't know what it is," he said and met my eyes.

"It's like lightning running through your veins, and there's nothing you can do to try to ignore it," I murmured.

"Blue lightning," he said and leaned in close enough to rest his head on my shoulder. "What do we do now?"

"You take me home so I can get some clothes on. Then we see what we can find out. There has to be something online or someone has to know something. We can't be the only two people to experience what we have. The voice has to belong to whoever else is involved. I think we should try to figure out who that person is and what they want."

He pulled back enough to look at me and shook his head. "I can't believe I once again got sidetracked about getting you some clothes. Let's go then. Once you're feeling better, I'm more than willing to see what we can find out. But I do think it's important you rest. I have a feeling there is way more to this than we know."

"I'll make an appointment with my doctor as soon as possible. I want to know everything is okay too. And I'm sorry I put you in the position I did at the hospital, but I had to get out of there." The lightning had hit me once, what if I was hit again? What if I was inside? What would happen to everyone who was near me? I couldn't take that chance. Not until I knew exactly what was happening.

After releasing my hand, he patted my arm. "Let's get you home."

I settled back in the seat and neither of us spoke until we passed the city limits sign to Hickory Crossing. "Go through the four-way stop and turn at the first left." He followed my directions, and, in a few minutes, we pulled up in front of my house. It looked exactly the same as it had when I'd left this morning even if I wasn't the same. "Thanks again," I said, and wasn't sure if he'd be following me in or not. But he rushed around to my side to help me out.

"Let me at least make sure you make it through the door," he said.

I nodded, not able to think of a single reason why I wouldn't want him to help me. I stepped out of the van and without looking I knew the burns on my feet were also healed but I didn't want to throw more at Bobby than I already had, so I kept my mouth shut and let him guide me to the house. Opening the door, I stepped inside, and Clawd, my black cat, gave me a glance before going right back to sleep with a stretch of his front foot.

"Right then, I'll be going," Bobby said as he turned to walk away.

"No wait." I held myself back from rushing over to where he stood on the front walk.

"Are you okay?" he asked and took a step toward me.

"I'm not ready to be alone," I admitted.

He paused a moment before nodding and walking back to where I stood just inside the door. "Then I'll stay," he said, and closed the door behind him.

EIGHT

Bobby

AFTER SETTLING ON THE couch next to a big black cat that completely ignored me, I turned on the television with the remote Cole had shoved into my hand before he hurried off to shower. His house looked like any other house I'd been in. A few pictures on the wall, a big flat screen, and a sofa with a built-in recliner at each end.

"Who the fuck are you?" a woman asked as she walked into the house without even so much as a knock. She had the same bright blue eyes Cole had but her hair was not as dark as his. She was also barely five feet tall when he was closer to six feet. But what she lacked in height she made up for in attitude. She had lots and lots of attitude. "Well? You better start talking. Don't think I can't knock you on your ass."

"I-I," I stammered as I tried to form a coherent sentence but apparently the day *had* actually gotten to me, and this was the breaking point. Leaping to my feet, I wasn't sure what to say or where to go. Here I was a stranger in a stranger's house being confronted by someone who obviously belonged.

"Mom! What are you doing?" Cole said as he hurried to stand between us wearing only a towel. "I could hear you yelling over the shower."

"I walked in, and this guy was sitting on your couch like he owns the place," she yelled again.

"Mom, this is Bobby—" He trailed off and looked at me.

"Sanders, Bobby Sanders," I managed to get out.

"Bobby saved my life," Cole said. Her gaze bounced from him to me before she pulled him into her arms and hugged him.

"Oh, baby, are you okay?" She released him enough to meet his eyes, it was then I noticed he'd shaved his head.

"Yes, just a few burns. My hair was singed so I shaved it off."

"Wait a minute, what happened?" she said.

"Bobby, this is my mom, Marie Ryan," Cole said while she continued to hold onto him.

"What happened?" she asked again before finally releasing him.

"Give me just a minute to put on some pants," he said and hurried out of the room after giving me a cringy look.

When I looked back at his mum, she had her arms crossed and huffed at me. I wondered if she thought I was also the reason he'd been hurt but there wasn't a chance in hell I was going to ask.

"So, this morning when I was out for my run, I got hit by lightning," Cole said as he walked back into the room pulling a shirt down over his toned abs that I was trying like hell to ignore.

"What? How could that happen?" she asked and checked him all over for injuries which I now noticed were no longer visible. "Is that what happened to your hair?"

"There was a storm in the distance, and it rolled in faster than I was running. Bobby was driving and saw it all. If he hadn't been there, I'd probably still be in the ditch. And my hair was half burned, there was no saving it, and I was tired of the smell of burnt hair."

She looked at me then, and I braced myself for whatever reaction she had this time, but surprisingly she pulled me in for a hug. "I'm so sorry for the way I treated you. I had no idea Cole had been injured. Now tell me everything," she said, and took a seat on the couch.

He guided me back to where I'd been sitting when she came in and listened while he told her what had happened. It never got easier to hear, and it was just as fresh in my memory as it had been when I'd seen it a few hours ago.

"You need to go to a hospital," his mum said.

"Bobby took me to Woodland. But—something weird happened, and I made him bring me home."

"What do you mean? Cole, none of this makes any sense." She again looked between the two of us looking for more answers that neither of us had.

"I know. I don't really know what happened either. The doctors were checking me out and it was almost like I was hit by lightning again. Or lightning came to me. I don't really know how to explain it."

I sat in silence, unsure if Cole wanted me to say anything, and not wanting to either upset his mum or tell her something he didn't want her to know. Not that either of us knew what should be kept secret and what wasn't important. Neither of us knew what had happened or understood what could come from it.

"Is that what you saw?" she asked me.

"He was covered with a blue glow and sparks of lightning. But it sounded like there was a tornado going through the hospital so maybe it wasn't what we thought it was. Maybe it was a micro storm or something." I knew that wasn't what happened but the more I thought about it the more I doubted it all.

She flinched away from me before turning back to Cole. "What's he talking about?"

"We don't know what happened, but things definitely got weird at the hospital. Once we left it hasn't been quite so crazy." He glanced at me when he said it and I knew he was hoping I didn't mention the fact that the blue glow had tried to move from his skin to touch me.

"What did the doctor say?" she asked.

"We didn't stick around to find out. Like I said, it got weird."

"You need to see a doctor," she said and looked him over once again. It was strange to see his head shaved, but it was also more obvious how singed he'd been. His hair was burned all the way to his scalp in some areas, and red marks showed where he'd nearly been burned, but even those had faded since we'd left the hospital.

"I'll make an appointment for as soon as they can get me in. Mom, there's more," he said and once again glanced at me. "When we were at the hospital, I heard something. I don't really know how to describe it without you thinking I'm nuts."

"What did you hear?" she said, her voice low and serious.

"With a flash of blue—"

"There will be two," I continued. His mum looked between the two of us as the color drained from her face.

"It can't be," she said and stood and walked out the door leaving the two of us alone.

NINE

Cole

MY MOM'S REACTION SHOCKED me and told me she knew something. But it couldn't have been about the lightning because how could she?

"Do you think she knows something?" Bobby asked, still looking at the door like he expected her to come bursting through it again.

"I'm sorry for her reaction when she got here. I heard her from the bathroom," I said, changing the subject.

He shrugged before looking at me. "She doesn't know me. I can't imagine my reaction if I walked into my parents' house and found a stranger on the couch, and they were nowhere to be seen."

"I think you may be right. She had the oddest look on her face when I told her what I'd heard." It wasn't shock, the look on her face was more like recognition. Bobby stood again from where he'd been on the couch and walked toward the door.

"I think I should go, I don't want to cause any trouble," he said as he reached for the doorknob.

"No, I don't want you to go." I rushed over to him and wrapped my arms around his arm. Not to hold him there, but to experience the closeness of him again.

The lightning I felt just under my skin slowly moved toward his arm as the two of us watched. "There is definitely a connection between us," I said without looking away.

"But how can that be, we never knew each other until today."

"Probably the same reason you just happened to be driving on that road the exact same time I got struck by lightning. It can't all be coincidence."

He drew in a deep breath and relaxed against me. I could feel his anxiety diminish and his calm take over. *How can this be?* His voice in my head surprised me and I pulled back to look at him, but his eyes were not on me, and I knew he hadn't spoken, yet somehow, I had heard him.

The connection I feel to him makes no sense. His inner voice was different than his outer voice. Softer and smoother with an accent that told me just how Irish he really was.

"I feel our connection too, and I don't understand it. But something tells me it's okay," I said and forced myself to ignore the fact I'd heard his thoughts.

"Maybe I shouldn't question it so much, but this is all so strange. I'm going to go, but I'd like to speak again if you don't mind. I'm willing to do what I can to find out more."

"Don't change a thing. We don't know what we're dealing with and it's smart to be cautious. I'm going to call my doctor and see when they can get me in."

"Let me know when your appointment is, I'd like to go if you don't mind."

"I wouldn't mind at all." We exchanged phone numbers and when he moved to the door to leave, the energy in me pulled me closer to him, but I ignored it. He was dragged into this by chance, the same way I was, and both of us would need to decide how deeply we were involved.

Once he was gone, I leaned against the door and blew out a deep breath. "What the fuck just happened?" When I'd left my house this morning, I was filled with the monotonous dread of knowing this day would end like all the others had. But more had happened in the past few hours than had ever happened to me.

"Fuck." I was supposed to work today, Brian, the owner, was on vacation, and he'd put me in charge. Looking down I realized I wasn't dressed for work. Hurrying back to my bedroom I changed into work clothes before searching around for my phone. Remembering I'd had it in the living room, I hurried back out and realized just how lucky I was that I hadn't taken it on my run. I dialed the store before pulling on a shirt and ignored the fact I had so many scratches and abrasions on my face.

"Brian's Sporting Goods," Trina said, and I was never more thankful for giving her a set of keys in case she was there either early or late.

"Trina, this is Cole."

"Oh, hey, Cole, I thought you were working today." Her voice was calm and professional with not even a hint of panic. She was just out of high school but more professional and a harder worker than past employees who were twice as old as her.

"I am. I had a little accident on my run. I'll be right in, give me about ten minutes."

"No worries," she said and after briefly filling me in on a few items we needed to order, I was out the door and on my way to work.

The day was bright and sunny with not a cloud in sight, but there was a chill in the air that had nothing to do with the weather, which was actually very warm. More than half the day was already gone, and I wondered how I'd even made it this far. "I got struck by lightning," I said to myself and tried to wrap my mind around it once again. Anxiety started to bubble up in me, and if I hadn't been so close to work, I would have pulled over. As it was, I pulled into the parking lot and turned my car off just as my phone rang.

"Hello," I said without looking and took a deep breath.

"Where are you?" a voice I already recognized said. *Bobby.*

"I'm at work. I completely forgot I was supposed to work today, the owner is out of town this week so I can't just leave it." It never crossed my mind that I should question his call, somehow, I just accepted he knew I needed help and called.

"I could feel your anxiety. At first, I thought it was my own, but it was the same feeling I had earlier." His voice was very calm as he explained this very strange sensation to me, and I wondered for what had to be the millionth time how he could deal with this and not be freaking the fuck out and never speaking to me again.

"It all just sort of hit me. I was struck by lightning. I could have died," I admitted. "I know it could happen, but I didn't want to believe it could have happened to me."

"I thought you were dead when I first walked up to you. You were smoking," he whispered, and I knew this was almost as traumatic for him as it was for me.

"Can we meet later?" I hadn't meant to ask, but I missed him, and it had only been a short while since he'd left. I checked the time on my phone and was shocked it hadn't even been an hour. "Sorry, are you home yet?"

"Not yet. I made my delivery and I'm nearly there. And yes, I would like to see you later. What time are you done?"

"Six, I can meet you closer to your town if you'd like."

"Why don't we meet in Woodland, it's about the same distance for us both," he said. After deciding on a location, we said our goodbyes once again, and I hung up. Secure in the knowledge that in a few hours we'd be together again, while still wondering how this complete stranger could have become so important to me in half a day.

TEN

Bobby

I SAT IN THE work van where I'd pulled over just before I called Cole. His thoughts were a jumble filled with anxiety and confusion when he'd first answered, and I had no clue how I knew that. Before this morning, I had no clue who Cole Ryan even was, now there was a part of me that knew him better than I knew anyone.

With a flash of blue . . . The words continued to repeat in my mind. It wasn't Cole's voice that I heard, and it definitely wasn't mine. But the strange voice continued over and over, only just loud enough for me to hear when

I concentrated on it. Turning up the radio, I concentrated on driving, and forced myself *not* to focus on it.

I was finally focusing on the music when a call came through. "Hey, where are you?" Dad asked.

"I'm just going through Yuba City." I'd decided to go the other way around and avoid all reminders of going to the hospital earlier. So far that hadn't worked at all and had just given me a longer drive back to the shop.

"You were able to make the delivery?"

"Yeah, no problem at all. I was late but they didn't mind. They were just happy to get their order."

"Oh, good thing, Bobby. When you get back, I need your help on a big order for the casino." He was focused on work and not where I'd been earlier, which was fine with me, but I knew he'd be asking for more details once I was at the shop, and we were working.

"Sounds good. Sorry to be so late today," I said, because I knew it needed to be addressed.

"It's alright. I can't fault you for helping someone." Dad was always a good man. He'd stop and help anyone who had broken down on the side of the road no matter what their vehicle looked like or how scary they might have looked to someone else. He always said not to judge anyone by how they looked or what they drove, and I lived the same way. If someone needed help, I helped them.

"I'll fill you in on it all when I get back to the shop. It's been a wild day already."

"It's barely past noon and it sounds like you've had quite the adventure." He chuckled.

"Oh, you just wait until you hear about it," I said and smiled at his words.

"Alright, son, back to work, I'll see you soon."

"See you soon." I turned up the radio to a normal volume and after speaking with Dad I was able to relax more than I had been able to before. I focused on the music and not much else as I drove past the flat fields and pastures that would soon lead me to the small town of Sugarfield. It might have been small, but we were close enough to Sacramento and the airport for that to not really matter.

Sugarfield had started out as a rural area of Woodland where a sugar factory processed the local sugar beets. But eventually as Woodland grew, so had Sugarfield. It was nice here, not too country to be in the middle of nowhere, but country enough to know all your neighbors. I waved to a few familiar faces as I drove to the shop, and finally pulled into the parking lot.

The giant Print 4 You sign with a pointing finger was affixed to the roof and even though we took most orders online or by phone, we were easy enough to find if anyone needed to.

"I'm back," I yelled as I walked into the copy room where all the machinery was located and over to where Dad was standing next to one of the machines getting it set up for a run.

"Oh good, we just got another big order." He handed me the paperwork while I handed him the workorder from earlier. Both of us paused to read before moving off to do what was needed.

I glanced at the order and the proof. "Well, this is different," I said and grinned at Dad.

"Yeah, we don't get many orders for carnival flyers."

"We get none that I've seen." I read the proof announcing the Carnival of Mysteries would soon be coming to Hickory Crossing for one weekend only and listing all the performers and entertainment that would be included in your low admission price. "Do people go to carnivals anymore?"

"Sure they do," Dad said. "There just aren't as many as there used to be."

"Yeah, I guess." I walked over to the machine I'd be printing from and after downloading the image and setting it all up, I got busy printing off the five hundred flyers they'd ordered.

"So, tell me what happened earlier," Dad said as he walked over to where I stood checking everything was set up right for the print run.

"Well, I was driving to Hickory Crossing—" I continued for the next twenty minutes until I'd told him everything. "It feels like it happened a month ago, but at the same time as if it was a few minutes ago. I can still smell how he smelled like burnt hair and clothes, but it was electrical burns, so it was tinged with a sour smell."

"That guy is lucky to be alive. I can't believe you saw him get hit, or that he survived." Dad's eyes were wide, and I knew the exact emotions he was feeling. I'd felt them over and over today. "He really should have stayed at the hospital. What if he has internal injuries? It's very common for the lightning to do a lot of damage to the internal organs." Dad knew a little bit about everything, and I wasn't surprised he knew something about being struck by lightning. "How did he seem when you left him?"

"He took a shower, shaved his head, and he seemed fine."

Dad stared at me for a full minute before shaking his head. "It's hard to believe he could just get up and go to work without any issues."

"There's more," I said, because there was no way I was going to tell him all the crazy shit I'd seen today, but I had to tell him enough to find out more information if he had it. "When his mum came over to check on him, he told her he'd heard something when he was struck."

"He heard something. Like a noise?"

"More like a voice. With a flash of blue. That's what it said. When he told his mum, she looked like she'd been slapped. It was obvious she knows more, but she left almost as soon as he said it."

He rubbed his chin as he thought about what I'd said. "I've never heard that before. Did you google it to see if you had any luck?"

"No, I hadn't really had time to think about it."

"Let me see what I can find out," he said, and turned back to the job he'd been working on.

"Thanks, I'm meeting Cole later. I really want to make sure he's okay."

"Bobby, be careful. I don't want anything to happen to you either."

"What could happen to me?" I asked, but then I thought about how Cole looked being thrown through the air and my mouth went dry. "I'll be careful."

Eleven

Cole

Work was busy, and I was never so thankful for a big order to put away as I was today. A few people noticed my hair, but I just said that it was time for a change, and I shaved it on a whim. The singe marks on my arms and abrasions on my face were harder to ignore or explain, but the more serious burns had all healed and faded to nothing more than pink marks. Mostly I gave vague excuses about me tripping and falling while on my morning run. Because they all knew I ran.

I was busy stocking up the hiking boots when the door chime sounded, and I looked up to see Miss Avery. *Fuck.* "Cole?"

"Oh, hey, Miss Avery, how are you?" She never came in here unless she needed something, and I knew this had more to do with this morning than her needing a new pair of shoes.

"I came to see how you are. I was just at the grocery store and noticed you through the window. Are you sure you're not hurt?"

"What do you mean?" I asked and looked away because I knew exactly what she meant.

She walked close enough to grab my arm, and I noticed her freakishly strong grip. I didn't know how old she was, but it had to be at least in her seventies. She had lived alone on her farm as long as I'd been alive, and still managed to plant her crops and tend her goats with help from a hired hand or two. But most of the work she did on her own. Including milking her herd of goats. "I saw you get struck by lightning. I was just on my way out to check if you were injured when I saw a van pull up and a strange guy load you up. I was worried he might be trying to take advantage of you, so I wrote down the name of the company just in case."

"He took me to the hospital, and they checked me out. There was nothing seriously wrong other than a bit of singed hair and skin." I grinned and hoped it would come out lighthearted while inside I was freaking out. I didn't want anyone to know what had happened if I could avoid it. But I wasn't sure why it even mattered.

She leaned in close, while Trina peeked around the corner before backing away and making herself busy with something else. "There is no way you weren't hurt. You were thrown at least ten feet and landed hard. I saw smoke coming off you when you landed."

"I guess I got lucky," I said with a shrug.

"With a flash of blue," she mumbled barely loud enough for me to hear.

"What was that?" I asked and hoped she didn't say another word.

"Nothing. Just something I remember from a long time ago." She had a faraway look in her eyes and for a moment I stared at her staring off into the past, or the distance, I wasn't sure which.

"Sorry, but I've really gotta get back to work. I came in late because of going to the hospital so I want to make sure I get everything done before closing time."

"Oh, sorry, Cole. I understand. Please let me know if you need anything. I'm so relieved to know you weren't injured." Without another word she walked out the way she'd entered. Full speed ahead, head held high, and full to the brim with confidence.

"You really did get struck by lightning?" Trina asked, her eyes wide.

"Yeah, but it wasn't as bad as it probably looked. I mean I did get a little banged up but nothing serious."

"Except burnt hair. You still smell like burnt hair," she said.

I reached up and scrubbed my hand over my newly short hair and after smelling my hand I agreed, I did smell like burnt hair. "Hopefully that goes away soon."

Trina burst out laughing making her eyes light up in humor. "Hopefully, or you'll be scaring the customers."

"Does it smell that bad?"

"Well, I can smell it, but I have a sensitive nose." She laughed again. "I'm sure it's fine and I really am happy you weren't hurt worse."

"Me too. I was lucky Bobby was driving along at the same time. I'm not sure what I would have done if he wasn't there." I knew I wouldn't have been able to walk back to town, I was at least five miles out, and the only other house in that area was Miss Avery. I guess I would have tried to make it there. "What was that?" I asked Trina when I realized she was waiting for me to answer something I hadn't heard.

"I said that was lucky. I don't even want to think about how badly you could have been hurt."

"Yeah, well Brian will be back next week, and we'll be back to normal before then."

"Sure thing, Cole." She walked back to where she'd left a few boxes of running shoes someone had tried on earlier and got back to work.

My mind was a mess of Bobby, and blue lightning, and so many questions about both. I'd googled his business since I'd seen it on the side of the van and there was no way I'd forget that. It was just like he said, a family-owned printing business in Sugarfield that had opened recently after expanding from another office in Dublin.

There was a picture of his family, and I couldn't bring myself to stop looking at him. He wore a big smile like the rest of his family. His blond hair was a little longer and he was tanned, but other than that he looked exactly the same. Unable to stop myself I sent him a text asking where he wanted to meet. We'd said we'd meet in Woodland, but he hadn't said where.

> *What do you think of meeting in old town, and we can decide then?*

he sent back almost immediately.

> *That sounds great, I'll be there around six-thirty.* I was off at six and I planned to get everything done before then and be ready to leave.

> *I can't wait to see you.*

Reading his reply, once again, the strange connection we had pulled at me, and I wondered if he felt it too because even though I didn't send another text, I knew he knew I felt the same way. Only a few more hours until I'd see him again, and I hoped he didn't think it was weird that we had this connection. Because I wasn't sure what would happen if he wasn't there, at the other end of the blue glowing cord that connected us.

TWELVE

Bobby

I'D FINISHED THE PRINT job Dad had given me and printed off a few extras to show Cole. I wasn't exactly sure why, but I wanted to show him. It wasn't anything special, just an old-fashioned carnival. The kind that typically showed up in every small town down the interstate all summer long. Dad had researched the strange line that Cole and I both somehow now knew but didn't find out much about it.

"It's something the sun does when it's setting, or sometimes when it's rising over water. I doubt that has anything to do with this," he said.

"No, I don't think so either. I'm meeting Cole soon, and I want to ask if we can speak with his mother because I would bet she knows more."

"Just be careful, son. You don't know these people, and I don't want to see something happen to you." His eyes were filled with worry, and he squeezed my shoulder. I appreciated his concern, and the fact he didn't try to talk me out of going, just cautioned me.

"I will. His mum was sort of scary. While he was in the shower, she walked into his house and I was waiting for him, and I think she thought I had broken in. For a tiny woman she's terrifying." Dad laughed at that and patted me on the back.

"Just be careful."

"I will," I said and finished work for the day.

I took the exit that would take me right into the old town area of Woodland. There were quite a few choices of places to eat down here that weren't the usual restaurant chain places. I found a parking space near where we'd decided to meet at the corner of Elm and Main. After turning off the engine, I sat in silence as the engine creaked and groaned while cooling off.

Closing my eyes I thought of Cole, and how strange it had been earlier. It seemed like a whole other day, or week, that it had all happened, but in reality, it had only been a few short hours ago. Less than a day.

A feeling scratched at my skin. The sensation of electricity crawling up my arm after touching my finger to a wall socket. Yes, I was that kid that had to find out what happened if he shoved a fork into the socket. It did not end well, and I never tried it again. But I remember that sensation. I remembered it like it had happened yesterday.

I opened my eyes to find Cole standing in front of my car, and I would have sworn I could see the blue glow around him. I hurried to where he stood and held my hand out to shake his, but he surprised me by pulling me in for a hug. "You're too important for only a handshake," he whispered in my ear.

I held him close before pulling back just enough to meet his eyes without releasing his arms. "Is everything okay?

You're feeling good?" My eyes danced all over him looking for any changes since I'd left him, but he looked the same. If anything, the redness around his abrasions had faded.

"No, I'm fine. Actually, I feel great. How about you?"

I took a step back then and shoved my hands in my pockets. "Yeah, I'm good. Just still really confused about what happened. But I'm so glad you're okay. I was worried you would cancel, or you'd tell me you were not doing as well as you had been." The words rushed out of me but all of them were true, and Cole made me want to be honest and open with him. We'd shared something strange that not many people had even seen or experienced, and I guessed that was what bonded us.

"I wouldn't have cancelled. I've been thinking about you all afternoon," he said as we crossed the street, making me smile and release some of the tension I hadn't realized I was carrying.

"My dad googled the blue flash thing but didn't find out anything," I said.

"Yeah, you mentioned that earlier." He gave me a questioning look and I knew I was rambling nonsense.

"Sorry."

Cole stopped walking and rested his hand on my arm. "Nothing about this is normal. I kept waiting for either lighting to strike me or for my heart to stop beating. I looked up what happens when you're struck by lightning, and I really fucking wish I could forget what I read."

He was so vulnerable, and so willing to admit his fears and challenges. I hadn't met anyone like him before, and I hoped we would last longer than tonight, but I wasn't confident we had enough in common to make it past dinner. Both of us were uncomfortable, and between the few words we spoke the silence stretched out for miles.

"Let's try this place," Cole suggested. It was an old-fashioned café that had been here for as long as I can remember. It served typical café food with the dinner combinations of a main dish with two sides, salads, and lots of sandwiches. We walked in and immediately I felt comfortable.

"Good choice," I said and finally met his eyes. We were told to choose a seat so we walked back to the corner where we could talk without everyone listening. It was still a small town and people loved their gossip.

We both picked up the menus that were already on the table and chatted about what we'd choose. Some of the discomfort I'd felt earlier started to fade, and it started to feel more like a first date than two people meeting to talk about a shared experience. I still wasn't sure how I felt about Cole. He was nice enough, but it bothered me that he was so calm about everything, and his mother—she definitely knew more.

"Bobby? What did you want?" Cole said. The waiter had walked over to take our order and I hadn't even noticed.

"Sorry, I'll have the chicken fried steak." After Cole ordered we were once again alone, and just like earlier, conversation failed us. His hand rested on top of the table and brushed closer to mine when he shifted in his chair.

Blue sparks flew from his fingers to mine. Not a lot, but just enough for me to see, and for both of us to feel. My eyes met his and I knew we'd need to figure this out. We might suck at trying to get to know each other, but something wanted us to figure it out, and it didn't seem ready to give up on us just yet.

Thirteen

Cole

We were both uncomfortable tonight, it was easy enough for anyone to see, but once the spark left my finger and touched his, it ignited that connection again. "Something wants us together," I whispered.

"I think so too," Bobby said, his eyes fixed on the narrow space between our hands.

"I'm sorry things have been so awkward," I said, and met his eyes. "I really was looking forward to seeing you again." His green eyes were focused only on me, and I wanted to do whatever it took to keep him interested.

"Maybe we just built it all up too much," he said, but finally grinned. "I was looking forward to seeing you too."

"I want to think there's more to my attraction to you than one shared experience. Why don't we try to figure out exactly what happened, and we'll see where we go from there," I said and waited for his response.

He smiled then and reached across the table to cover my hand with his. "I'd like that. Because I really do want to know what happened, and I want to get to know you better. Because no matter how I try to fight it, I do feel drawn to you."

Our food arrived then, and we ate like we hadn't eaten all day, and in my case that was true. I'd skipped my lunch-break because I got to work so late. Now I was starving, and this had to be the best chicken parmesan I'd ever eaten in my life. "How's yours?" I asked between bites.

"Great. I skipped lunch so I could finish that print order."

"Same, I felt bad going in so late." We both laughed. We were more alike than either of us was ready to admit. But spending time with him like this was what I needed. Just to know that he was real, and he was a regular guy who also happened to be a good person was enough for me.

"Oh, I almost forgot," I said and wiped my mouth. "One of the property owners that lives out that way saw what happened."

"What did they say?"

"Not much. Miss Avery was in town and stopped by to see if I was okay. She said she saw you pick me up and was worried at first, but she knew I needed help. She did write down the name of your company just in case I came up missing." I smiled at him over my forkful of food.

"She saw everything?" Bobby asked.

"I think so, but she didn't mention any details. Just said she knew I needed help."

"I'm relieved that someone else noticed. Cole, I can't explain how shocking it was. I know we've both tried to minimize it, but it really was bad." He leaned in close and glanced around before he spoke again. "What happened at the hospital is something else we need to look into."

I set my fork down, the thought of it taking my appetite. "I could have died so easily, and I still don't know what happened there. Or why I said that poem or whatever it was."

"What if it was some sort of spell or a warning?" Bobby said, and once again settled his hand over mine. The energy between us buzzed in the happy way it seemed to when we were close enough to touch. "I hope you don't mind. I like touching you."

"I don't mind, I like your touch too. A spell?"

"Yeah, like magic. I don't really know, but what you said at the hospital didn't sound like a poem. It was more than that."

"I hadn't thought of that," I said before taking another bite of food, my nerves now forgotten.

"Did you get a chance to talk to your mum?"

"Not yet. I don't see my parents every day, but I do see them a few times a week. If I don't hear from her tomorrow, I'll go after work and talk to her." She knew something. Whether she just recognized the poem, or spell, or whatever it was, or she really did know more, remained to be seen.

"Let me know what she says. So far, she's the only one that seems to know anything."

"I will, and I agree. Although Miss Avery acted very strangely when she came into the store. But I guess there isn't really a normal way to check on someone you saw get struck by lightning." I huffed out a laugh and he grinned at me.

"No, there really isn't. I think my dad thought I was joking when I told him about it, but when I told him we'd been to the hospital he knew it was serious."

"If someone told me what happened I'd feel the same way. It's different when you experience it." I thought back to this morning and just before I'd been struck. It was just like any other day, until—

"What do you remember?" Bobby asked.

"I was running. I had just run past Miss Avery and waved hello to her when I saw the clouds start building to the east, so I picked up my pace. I was about five miles out of town, and I knew I wouldn't be able to make it back before it started pissing down rain on me." He grinned at my use of the word he'd have used if he were still in Ireland. "Out of the corner of my eye I would have sworn I saw the clouds illuminated in blue. That same electric blue that the sparks are. I turned to look and that's the last thing I remember. Then you were waking me up."

"It's probably better you don't remember. It had to be painful," Bobby said.

"Possibly. When I regained consciousness all I felt was numb. The way your hand feels after you touch the prong on a plug by mistake as you're plugging it in."

"I know that feeling well."

"When we were on the way to the hospital my body seemed to clench up. All my muscles seized up and I had no control over myself."

"That must have been when you had the seizure."

"I don't think it was a seizure," I said. "I think the lightning was changing my body and making it into what it needed."

"What? How could you know that? Is—is that even possible?" Bobby whispered and stammered as he struggled to understand.

"The voice in my head told me, it keeps telling me lots of things. Some of it I can block out, but not all of it. It's always there, and always talking. Bobby, I'm afraid," I whispered and leaned in closer to him. His eyes met mine and I knew he was looking for any deceit, but I'd never been more honest or serious in my life.

He reached across the table and cradled my cheek in his hand. "I'm not going anywhere. I promise. I'll help you any way I can." He meant it, he meant every word, and finally I really was able to relax knowing I wouldn't be going through whatever the fuck this was by myself.

FOURTEEN

Bobby

LIFE WENT ON. AFTER Cole and I had gone out that night, we hadn't seen each other in person. It had been two weeks. We messaged each other daily and some days we spoke on the phone. But the longer I was away from him, the more the pull to him seemed to fade. Life went on.

Driving to a delivery I got a text notification and smiled when I saw it was Cole.

> *Just checking to see how you're doing.*

I waited until I pulled into the parking lot of the business I was delivering to.

> *Hey, things are good. Work is crazy, which I guess is good. How are you?*

> *I'm good. Glad the boss is back. I'm more than happy to just be the manager.*

I laughed at that. I understood more than I could even explain. My dad had wanted me to take over this location so he could start another in Sacramento, but I was honest and told him I wasn't really cut out for that, and didn't think I was the best fit.

While he appreciated my honesty, I knew he was disappointed but not as disappointed as he'd have been if the business failed because I wasn't able to keep all the balls in the air.

> *I'm happy to stay an employee and do what I'm told. Not sure I'm cut out to be the boss.*

I watched as he stopped and started his reply a few times. It was strange, we'd only seen each other one day, but there was a part of me that missed him. Call it instant attraction, or possibly that weird thing when you meet a stranger and feel like you've known them forever. Whatever it was I did want to see him again, but I was also afraid that same intense feeling that told me to stay with him at all costs would take me over again. Those feelings had faded, and now I thought of Cole as a friend.

Let's figure out a time we can get together. I really have missed you.

His raw honesty did strange things to me and made me realize those feelings hadn't faded nearly as much as I wanted to think they had.

When is good?

I tapped out before I had a second to think better of it.

How is Friday?

A thought hit me, and I tapped out a reply.

That sounds great. There's a carnival that's going to be outside of Woodland this weekend. We could check it out.

I had zero clue what the carnival was or if he even liked that sort of thing. But the flyer had stuck with me, and it sounded like a good place to go that had food and entertainment. Plus, it was outside so we wouldn't have any awkward silence.

After tapping out the directions and what time I thought would work for both of us, he replied saying he'd see me there. I glanced in the mirror and was surprised to see myself looking so happy. I guess maybe it wasn't all imagined feelings after all. I couldn't wipe the grin off my face as I collected the order from the back of the van and walked up to the business to deliver it. Today was Monday, and I found I was more anxious than I would have expected to see Cole again.

"Wonder if he's as anxious," I mumbled as I pushed the door open.

"What was that?" the owner of the small restaurant asked as I walked up to the counter.

"Nothing, I have a delivery of menus for a Carmen Alvarez."

"How did it go?" Dad asked when I walked into the print shop and handed him the paperwork from the delivery.

"Good. She was very happy."

"That's what I like to hear." Dad moved over to one of the presses that was running a big order, and after checking the ink and paper were still good, he walked back over to me. "Have you heard from lightning boy?" he asked, using the nickname he'd come up with when he couldn't remember Cole's name. He hadn't asked me for about a week. Once he realized we weren't seeing each other all the time he'd backed off. Which I appreciated.

"I asked him if he wanted to meet me at the carnival we made flyers for."

"Did you? I was wondering if you were ever going to see each other again. It sounded like you had a lot in common."

"I wasn't sure I wanted to. I love chatting with him, but when we're together—" I cleared my throat before looking at anything but Dad.

"What is it?"

"I don't know. I'm just looking forward to seeing him again."

"You know, when I met your mother, it seemed there was no way we could end up together. We were from a world apart and we were both young. Neither of us could afford to fly back and forth. And this was before the age of cellphones and computers. But we made it work. We wrote each other letters."

"Real letters on real paper. You've told me this story a few times," I said and smiled at him.

"Sorry, I'm a sentimental fool. But you already know that. My point is, once I met your mother, no matter how much I tried to be her friend—I couldn't. There were too many emotions attached to her, and she made me happy."

"That's how I feel about Cole. At first, I thought I was attracted to him because we'd both shared such a strange experience, but not seeing him hasn't dimmed my feelings for him. He's a great friend, but somehow that word doesn't describe him."

"Go to the carnival and enjoy yourself. Forget about the way you met and see how you feel at the end of the night. Maybe you'll realize there wasn't as much there as you wanted there to be, or maybe you'll realize there's far more than just helping a guy who got struck by lightning." His eyes twinkled and I couldn't stop myself from grinning back at him.

"Okay, I'll see how it goes. But it's highly unlikely I can forget about the lightning."

"Do your best, son," he said and clapped me on the back. "Back to work, we got another order while you were out with that delivery."

FIFTEEN

Cole

A LOT HAD HAPPENED since I'd seen Bobby. But I wasn't sure I needed to tell him everything. Not because I wanted to keep secrets from him but because it was all really fucking weird, and I was having a hard time wrapping my mind around it all. I looked at the wall I'd made that had all the information I'd gathered.

"It looks like a crime scene investigation," I mumbled to myself as I continued to stare at it. In the center was the poem or whatever the fuck it was, I'd heard on repeat since that first day. I had managed to figure out a few things, but I still wasn't sure how it was all connected.

"Any luck?" Mom asked when she walked in a few minutes later. She folded her arms and stood looking at it all while standing next to me.

"Not really, but thanks for telling me all you did. It might end up helping more than we realize."

"You might try to find Nox; he could have more information about what happened that summer. He left town afterward, and I haven't seen him here since, but Anna Avery might be able to help you."

"Miss Avery?" I asked. We lived in a small town, but I had never once heard my mom mention anything about her.

"Yes, she's Nox's aunt."

"Tell me again what happened. I just can't believe all of this is connected, and I don't want to get anyone else involved until we know everything is connected." I thought about my plans to meet with Bobby and about all the chances I'd had the past two weeks to tell him what my mom had told me, but he was involved by chance, and I didn't want to tangle him in this mess any more than he already was.

She took a deep breath and glanced toward the door. I knew she was checking to see if Dad was there, but he was at work. They'd all been involved that summer, and she knew he wouldn't like the fact she was bringing it back up. "The summer we all graduated high school your father, Nox, and I spent a lot of time together. We'd all grown up here together, but until the last month of school none of us had been all that close. Egan and I had exchanged a few looks but nothing more. Just enough to let the other know we liked what we saw."

"Ew," I said, making her laugh.

"We weren't always this old," she said with a laugh.

"I know, go on," I encouraged her and forced myself not to grimace.

"Nox had always been quiet and a little weird. He seemed to prefer to be alone, and no one I knew had ever gone to his home or had him over to theirs. Don't get me wrong, Anna is lovely, but Nox's mother was not."

"Did he live with Miss Avery?"

"Not until after graduation. Then his mom just disappeared one night. Some of the townsfolk thought she had a secret lover in another town, but others thought Nox's father had returned and taken her with him, but I don't think either is what really happened." She gave me a look that made my blood run cold, and I struggled to say the words I knew she was thinking.

"You think she's dead," I finally managed to choke out.

She glanced down at the floor and drew her lips tight while drawing in a deep breath. "I'm not sure, but I know she didn't leave because she wanted to. That woman never left their house. She had Nox do the shopping and if he needed help Anna pitched in where she could, but something definitely wasn't right in their home. After she left Nox went to live with Anna, but like I said he left at the end of summer."

"You said the three of you were together more that summer."

"Yeah, we partied a little but mostly we tried to help him with a spell he was working on." Her eyes met mine then she waited for my reaction. When she'd first told me the story, I hadn't been sure what she was saying.

"He practiced witchcraft."

"Yes, or something like it. It wasn't like he had a book of magic or anything like that. He said a voice told him what to do and how to do it to gain more power."

"Was he schizophrenic?" I had no experience with mental illness, and for a while I thought that's what was making me hear the voice in my head, but now I wasn't so sure.

"No. There was nothing wrong with him, just like there's nothing wrong with you. The only difference is he was seeking the power, and he was being guided by a voice he managed to convince us would lead us to power and riches."

"What kind of power?" I asked.

"Well, teenage me didn't understand that part, but I did understand the riches part and to an eighteen-year-old who still wasn't sure where their life was going that sounded pretty good. Until we went to the carnival." Her eyes met mine then, and even though I'd heard this, it still made me nervous about hearing it again.

"When we first got there, we rode a few rides, ate some food, we even played a few games. But we soon realized the reason Nox wanted to go was to see the fortune teller. He had decided that she could tell him the way to follow the voices in his head and gain the power he wanted."

"Why did you and Dad go along with it? I mean he didn't make you go. You could have just left."

She shrugged her shoulder. "We were stupid kids and honestly, I was curious. I'd never been to a fortune teller, so I wanted to see what it was all about."

"Okay so tell me again what she said." I'd heard this a few times now, but it still creeped me out. I always thought of my parents as hard-working, logical people. Apparently not so much when they were younger.

"She was standing outside her tent when we walked by. Nox locked eyes with her, and it was almost like they were having a silent conversation. She nodded before walking over and holding the tent open for us. There was a table in the center of the tent, and I remember thinking how cheesy it was. But that was before she spoke. 'With a flash of blue.' "

SIXTEEN

Bobby

THE REST OF THE week was busy enough I didn't worry about Friday taking too long to arrive. I'd chatted with Cole a few times, and while I knew he was still trying to figure out the poem, he hadn't mentioned if he'd been able to find any information.

The radio played a song that reminded me of summer as I drove past the airport headed to where the carnival was being held. I tried to remember the last time I'd been to one, and while it had been a few years, it hadn't been so long that I forgot about the games and other attractions that made it fun. Or the corn dogs I was looking forward to eating while we were there.

The sun was just setting below the distant mountains when I exited the freeway and drove along the country road that led to the empty field where the carnival was set up. The tents and rides were visible from here, and I was excited to see what we'd find here, and to see Cole.

After paying to park I found a space on the far edge. I was willing to walk a little farther to get to the entrance rather than be stuck in traffic when everyone was trying to leave in a few hours. I tapped out a message to Cole as I walked toward the entry. The place was busy with lots of teenagers and families walking ahead of me.

"Hey," Cole said as he waved to me from just off the side of the entrance.

"Oh hey," I said and hurried over to give him a hug. He wrapped his arms around me, and for a moment neither of us moved. Finally, we both pulled away and shared an uncomfortable laugh. "Let's go see what's here."

Everything had a bit of an old-fashioned look, but it was also clean and well kept. Two men stood at the entrance; one was handing out tickets while the other stood nearby welcoming everyone, and he was dressed like what I imagined a ringmaster to be dressed like with top hat and boots. They were both hard not to stare at. The one handing out the tickets was tall with dark hair and dark eyes that seemed to see everything and more.

"Good evening, gentlemen," he greeted. "I hope you find the answers you're seeking while you're here." He met my eyes then and the intensity of his gaze shocked me. But as soon as the thought crossed my mind he looked away, and with a nod he moved on to the next person.

"What do you think he meant by that?" I asked Cole. His mind seemed to be elsewhere, and he paused before answering.

"Probably just something they say to sell the magic of the carnival," he said, but I could tell he didn't mean it. and the crease in his brow made me wonder what was bothering him. I glanced over my shoulder to see both men staring at us before one of them smiled at the other and they went back to greeting the next person in line.

"Should we wander around, or did you want to get something to eat?" I noticed a food stand at the end of the row that had a neon sign declaring they made the best corn dogs in the west. Again, he seemed distracted, but I wasn't sure what it was.

"A corn dog sounds good to me too," Cole said.

That cold feeling of dread slid down my back and I stopped in my tracks making him bump into me.

"Did you change your mind?" he asked.

"Cole, I never mentioned getting a corn dog … but I did think it."

His brow wrinkled in confusion as his eyes met mine. "No, I'm sure you mentioned it. You said something about the place on the end having the best—" His eyes widened, and he stared at me.

Can you hear me? I thought, and his eyes widened again before he slowly nodded.

"What does it mean?" he whispered as he started to tremble.

I pulled him over to the side next to a tent and put my back to the crowd so he was sheltered from the rush of people as much as I could manage. "Hey. Come here." I pulled him in for a hug and he clung to me. "Maybe this is what was meant to happen." He flinched in my arms and put his hand over one ear while pressing his other ear against my chest. "Are you okay?"

He shook his head. "It's not just your thoughts, I can hear everyone's thoughts. It's too much." I kept my arm around him and hurried over to where some tables were set up near a food vender and eased him into a chair. He rocked softly while clutching his head. He was so afraid and confused, but I wasn't sure how to help him other than being there for him.

The man from the entrance was walking down the aisle and glanced at us before walking over to where we sat.

"Is your friend injured?" he asked. I would have sworn he knew something was happening with Cole that went beyond normal as he stepped closer to him, his dark eyes filled with concern.

Cole looked up at him, and I could instantly tell he was better. The confusion and fear were gone. "I'm okay now. Thank you. I just had a bit of a panic attack. It's been a while since I've been around a crowd this size," he lied.

The man stared hard at Cole a moment longer before speaking. "You're sure you're, okay?"

"Yes, I'm fine now. Let's go walk around," he said to me.

"If you require medical assistance, please let one of the staff know," the dark-haired man said to me. After asking Cole once more if he was okay, he wished us a good night before disappearing back into the crowd of carnival goers.

"You're sure you're better?" I asked. He did look better, but I didn't know him well enough if he'd be honest about it or try to push through whatever it was.

"Yes. I was just a bit overwhelmed. But it's better now. I really would like to get something to eat and walk around," he said, and gave me a tentative smile.

We strode straight to the food stand I'd noticed earlier, and both of us ordered a corn dog and soda. He glanced around at all the brightly colored tents and attractions as though nothing strange had just happened. and he was deciding what to do next. I was at a loss for how to handle this situation. On the one hand I didn't want to bring it up if it had put him into a panic attack, but I wanted to know if it was true, and he could read minds.

He turned then and met my eyes. *It's true*, he said, but his lips hadn't moved, and he didn't look away as he waited for my reaction.

You can read my mind? I thought and didn't take my eyes off him as I waited to see what happened. He nodded before speaking.

"There's a lot I need to tell you, but I'm not sure this is the best place to do that. There's a power here I can feel but I'm not sure what it is." He glanced around again, but this time it didn't seem like a casual glance at all—he was looking for something or maybe someone.

"A power?" I whispered.

"Let's go sit down and eat." He took my hand like it was something we did all the time, and we walked with us both holding our food and drink in one hand, while he led us to the same area we'd just been, only now a few other people were gathered around tables eating whatever they'd chosen from the midway.

We found a small table and instead of sitting across from each other, he took the seat nearest my side. "I've found out quite a bit since the last time we saw each other."

"Why did you wait to tell me?" I asked, confused why he'd wait until now.

"I found out a lot, but I don't know what it all means or how it's connected. It's all very strange, and you were right. My mom did know something."

"Can you really hear my thoughts?" I whispered and leaned in closer to him.

"You and everyone else nearby. I think after tonight I'll need to be careful about where I go. If you weren't with me here, I wouldn't be able to handle being around this crowd. It's just too overwhelming." He spoke very quietly. So quietly I had to lean in to hear him.

"I haven't done anything," I said, confused how me being here helped him.

"The lightning chose you to be my north," he said like I should understand what he meant.

"What do you mean?"

"You know how one side of a magnet pulls another magnet to it, while the other side repels it? I think it's similar to that. When I was struck, the lightning chose you to be the one that could quiet the storm in my brain."

My mind raced as I tried to make any sense of his words, but then a memory hit me. The blue glow and spark of the lightning as it wrapped around him and reached for me. "The way it made me feel you," I whispered.

He nodded. "We're in this together whether we choose to be or not."

I took a deep breath and met his eyes again. There was no deceit, and I wondered if he was reading my mind now and waiting to see how I'd react to his words. "Tell me everything you found out."

SEVENTEEN

Bobby

WE SAT AT THE table while we ate our food and sipped our drinks. It was strangely normal in a situation that was nowhere near normal. But for some fucking reason I couldn't explain, I was more than willing to give Cole the time to explain it all to me. All while watching him a little too closely to be considered normal.

Cole looked around again and leaned in close to me. "Let's go out to the cars and we can talk out there," Cole said, and walked over to throw away his napkin and cup.

I threw mine away and when I met his eyes, he held out his hand. I took it without a second thought, and searched for that electric buzz I would forever associate with Cole. And blue. A flash of blue. Glancing his way while we walked, he seemed so at ease and comfortable.

"I'm fine now," he said as we hurried past the entrance and to my car. I wasn't sure why we chose it other than it was away from the other cars.

"Where did you park?" We'd met up near the entrance, but I didn't know what he drove, and hadn't seen him park. He pointed to a black SUV parked next to mine. "How did that happen?"

"Just lucky, I guess," he said.

"Or great minds think alike. I didn't want to get caught in traffic when we left."

He smiled but it didn't reach his eyes. "I'm sorry it's been so long since we've seen each other. There's been so much going on, and I didn't want to bring you into it if you didn't need to be. It's really a very strange story."

"Stranger than you being struck by lightning?" His eyes met mine and even in the dark car I could see how serious he was.

"Yes."

I looked out at the parking lot and over at the carnival where everyone was going on with their lives not even knowing about the strange circumstance we found ourselves in. So many thoughts ran through my mind, most of them to do with the fact Cole could now read minds. *What if he used that against me in some way?*

"I'd never do that. We'll find a way for you to close your thoughts to me. I don't know how I was able to mute everyone when we were in there, but if it hadn't happened, I think I would have lost my mind. There were a thousand voices all screaming different thoughts at me, but through all that I could focus on your mind, and it calmed me."

"What if we can't find a way? I don't like the idea that you can know everything I'm thinking." I tried to imagine a world where I would be okay with another person knowing my thoughts and I knew it wouldn't ever be okay. The lack of privacy, the lack of surprise. The fact he would know every memory I fought to forget and every bad experience I'd ever had that haunted me.

"Bobby, I promise you. I'm going to find a way to not invade your privacy. But I need to tell you what I've found out."

I took a deep breath and hoped to find an ounce of calm in this sea of confusion I was now plunged into. "Go ahead."

"My mom told me a story about when she was a teenager and had just graduated from high school. She and my dad had always known each other but they hadn't ever dated, and there was another guy who it seems was sort of an introvert. The other guy, Nox, was into some weird things that my parents didn't know anything about. But they were curious teenagers and went along with it until things got bad."

"I don't really understand what you're talking about."

He took another deep breath before continuing. "Nox was into witchcraft, or some sort of black magic. My parents helped him perform a few rituals, but they didn't know what they were doing, or what it really involved. They didn't take any of it seriously. Until he talked them into going to the carnival with him."

"What could have happened at the carnival?" I asked, but a part of me was afraid to know.

"They went to a fortune teller. Mom thought it was all a joke and didn't go in thinking it would change their lives. They walked into her tent and sat at her table. She asked them what they wanted to know. Nox said he wanted to know how to get more magic and more power. She shuffled her tarot cards, but before she could set them out her head was thrown back and she began to speak."

"What did she say?" I whispered, but I knew before he started.

"With a flash of blue there will be two. One of old and one of new. Wisdom and innocence must combine. If one of them is to remain alive," Cole said.

For a moment I didn't know how to react. "That's what you said at the hospital."

"That's what the fortune teller told them. My parents didn't know what it meant. But Nox did. Mom said he got more and more intense and started doing rituals that went from being fun and a little creepy, to deeply disturbing. She and Dad decided they didn't want anything else to do with Nox or whatever it was he was trying to do. They found out about a week later that he'd left town. His aunt didn't know where he'd gone and hadn't heard from him since then.

"Mom said they never tried to find him and were relieved when he left. She said in some ways she felt like he was controlling them somehow to get them to help with his rituals, but she didn't know that for sure."

"What does that have to do with what the fortune teller told them?" I asked.

"The ritual he was trying to do involved him being endowed with an ultimate power, a flash of blue," Cole said.

"Somehow you ended up with the power he was seeking."

"Yes, and I'm pretty sure he wants it."

"What do you mean?"

"The voice in my head is not my own, and I'm fairly sure it's his. Somehow, he's found a way to get in my head. I keep having horrible dreams so I'm not sleeping. I'm so on edge I feel like I could lose my mind."

"Can he hear your thoughts?" I asked.

"I'm not sure, but I think he can. I don't feel him there all the time so maybe it takes him some effort to get into my head."

"Oh, Cole," I said, and pulled him into my arms. He looked tired, but I'd put that down to the fact he was working a lot. I had no way of knowing he was being haunted in his dreams. "Does his aunt still live there? Maybe she can help."

"She does, and she was there when I got struck by lightning."

"The lady with the goats?"

"Yes."

"Have you talked to her?" I asked, and he shook his head.

"No, I don't know how to handle any of this. I'm really scared, Bobby. What if he tries to take this from me and it kills me?" he whispered.

I took his face in my hands, right now I didn't give a shit if he could read my mind or not, I wanted him to know he could count on me. "That's not going to happen. We'll find him and we'll stop him, but first we need to meet with the goat lady."

"Miss Avery," he said. His fingers encircled my wrist holding my hand to his cheek.

"We're going to meet with Miss Avery." I nodded to give that thought some emphasis, and he smiled but it didn't reach his eyes. He was terrified, and for the first time through all this crazy shit. I completely understood why.

EIGHTEEN

Cole

WE SAT A WHILE longer in the parking lot but really neither of us knew more than what we had shared while we sat and talked. "I should probably get going. I need to work tomorrow," I said. The week after my boss Brian returned from vacation, he'd gotten sick, and I'd been working more hours to make sure everything was taken care of.

"Cole, please call me if anything happens. When can we meet with Miss Avery?" Bobby asked.

I glanced at my phone for the time and seeing it was nearly ten I knew she'd already be in bed. "It's too late to call her tonight. I'll call her first thing tomorrow and see when she has time for us."

"Anytime this weekend is fine, or if it's next week, just let me know." He looked anxious and I tried not to listen to his thoughts, but it was incredibly hard to ignore. *I need to know you're safe.*

"I'll be careful. So far, I can hear his voice but mostly he repeats that poem. That's what I've heard all along. At first, I thought it was my mind trying to figure out its meaning, but then I realized it wasn't my voice. It's all so strange." I hadn't told my mom that, and Dad hadn't said one thing about Nox or that summer, and I didn't get the feeling he was all that willing to talk about it.

"I'm going to see what I can find out about blocking thoughts. Although I'm not really sure that's something I'll be able to find while searching online," Bobby said with a grin.

"Bobby, I swear I'll find a way to keep your thoughts private."

"How long have you been able to do this?"

"I've had whispers since it first happened. But the only voice I'd heard was what I now know was Nox. When we walked into the carnival though, it was like a slow building rain until it was a torrential downpour of thoughts. It was so overwhelming." That was putting it mildly. As soon as we passed through the entrance it was like being hit with a bucket of cold water or waking up from a long sleep and being fully awake.

Some voices were quiet murmurs while others were frantic shouts and all of it was way too overwhelming. But something made me hesitate to tell Bobby. I knew I could trust him, but he really didn't know me, and I guess I worried he'd think I'd lost my mind. Hell, *I* thought I'd lost my mind.

"Cole?" he said and settled his hand on my shoulder.

"Yeah, I'm okay. Sorry, I was just thinking."

"Hey, you told me you'd find a way to protect my thoughts and I'm telling you I will help you in any way I can. We'll start with meeting with Miss Avery. Let's see what she has to say. She might know nothing, or she might know how you can get rid of this power or at least control it."

He didn't mention the fact I'd been able to speak to him through his thoughts and I wasn't brave enough to bring it up. "You're right. I'll let you know what she says." I turned to reach for the door handle but his hand on my arm stopped me. When I turned back to him, he had leaned over closer to me.

"Is this okay?" he asked, before reaching up to cup my cheek in his hand. I could only nod in response. I tried to ignore his thoughts but the warmth there surprised me, and I was thankful to experience the emotions he equated with me. He leaned in and pressed his lips against mine. We'd never spoken about anything romantic between us, but his thoughts were colored with attraction that went beyond concern or friendship. "I've been thinking about kissing you all week," he admitted and pulled me close.

"You have?" I asked, before my brain caught up with my mouth. "I mean I didn't realize you felt that way for me." One thing was certain. I'd never been good at reading people, and this proved it. Even with the ability to read his mind I hadn't picked up on that attraction. To me it felt more like concern.

"Yes, I thought you would know with the mind reading thing," he said, and his expression softened. What I took for him not being interested was him holding back.

"I've never been known for being very attuned to other people. I expected you to think I was too old for you, or—I don't even know. I mean I'm really not all that exciting."

My face warmed as I blushed, and he grinned so big at me I couldn't hold back my own answering smile.

"You're not too old. I honestly hadn't even thought about that." His thumb gently glided over my cheek while he spoke, and I couldn't tear my eyes away from his green eyes.

"I love how your accent sneaks in at times. It's like finding a treasure when you're not even looking," I said. When he spoke, I found myself hoping it slipped through, but I noticed it only happened when he was either tired or stressed.

"I don't think of it much anymore. When I first moved here everyone would mention it, so I tried to soften it, but then I realized that was stupid and stopped. After all, my mother has a very strong Irish accent and mine comes out whenever we speak. So there really was no way I was getting away with leaving it behind."

"Don't try to hide it," I whispered, and when he leaned in again for another kiss, I settled my hand on the back of his head and pulled him in for a deeper kiss. His tongue met mine and the voices and madness in my mind went silent. He was all there was, and I wrapped my other arm around him hoping the silence continued.

When we broke apart the whispering was back, but I was too focused on him to care. "Get a room," a teenager yelled as he and a group of other teens walked behind the car, making both of us laugh.

"Totally worth it," Bobby said, and kissed my cheek.

"I should go, but I promise I'll call as soon as I set up a meeting."

"Sounds good," Bobby said, and we sat there a full minute staring at each other before leaning in for one more kiss.

"I'll talk to you tomorrow," I said, and without looking back this time I climbed out of the car. "Drive careful."

"You too," he said.

I opened my car door that was right next to his passenger side and started my car. I buckled my seat belt and checked my lights were on, and when I glanced over Bobby was watching me. I wanted him to look at me like that every day. And I wanted him close enough to silence the constant chatter that was now in my head.

The whispering in my mind returned, and I forced myself not to focus on it, but to focus on Bobby instead. It faded slightly and I hoped thinking of him always gave me the small relief it gave me right now. Because looking into his beautiful eyes gave me hope, and I decided I'd focus on that, not the feelings of dread and confusion that had taken over my mind. From now on, Bobby will be my focus. I waved goodbye to him and pulled out of the space, and we both drove out of the parking lot. He stayed behind me until we were at the freeway entrance then he turned to the left while I went to the right, my mind filled with the warmth of his kiss and the silence he'd temporarily granted me.

Nineteen

Bobby

The drive home seemed to take forever when it was actually less than thirty minutes. But when I pulled up to the small house that sat on my parents' property, I still wasn't ready to go inside. So many thoughts ran through my mind. Every one of them centered around Cole.

We'd only been together a few short hours tonight, but in that time, I felt like I found out more about him than I had in all the conversations we'd had. Most of the time we chatted it was just me asking if he was better, or him telling me he'd found out new information. There was more in that kiss than I expected. More emotion, and undeniably more connection.

Getting out of the car, I hurried to my door and let myself in. It was a good night. I thought back to Cole telling me he could read my thoughts. I still wasn't sure how to feel about it, and I definitely wanted to find out if there was possibly a way to block him. It wasn't so much that I didn't trust him. I just didn't think he needed to know more about me than I was willing to tell him.

My phone alerted me to a text, and I was happy to see it was from Cole.

> *I just made it home and I wanted you to know I had a great time tonight. I mean besides the whole . . . well you know what. I hope Miss Avery can see us tomorrow because I'll be counting down the days until we can see each other again. PS please don't think I'm being weird. I just really like you.*

I smiled as I read the words he'd written and imagined him tapping and deleting until he got it just right. He was older than me, and in some ways, he was more mature. But I didn't get the feeling he was any more experienced at relationships than I was. Which was really not at all.

I don't think you're weird. I think you're sweet, and I was just thinking about that kiss.

I nearly erased it but then I pressed send instead.

Goodnight Bobby xo

Goodnight Cole xo

The next morning there was a new text from Cole waiting for me then I checked my phone.

Cole: *I talked to Miss Avery. She can meet us later today. What time are you done with work?*

Bobby: *Good morning. Just let me know what time is good for you and I'll make it happen. We work today but the store isn't open.*

Cole: *I'm done at four. Want to meet me at the store?*

Bobby: *Sure, give me directions.*

Hickory Crossing was a small town, but I wasn't that familiar with it, so once he sent me a link to a map, I googled it to see what was there. Happy to know I'd see him soon, and I'd also get to see where he worked. There was a website for Brian's Sporting Goods, and smiled when I saw Cole pictured on the staff page.

He looked younger in the picture, and I remembered how long he'd worked there. Neither of us had really talked much about where we worked other than the bare minimum. But I wanted to know more about him, and I wanted to share more with him about me. And not with him reading my thoughts.

I googled that and found a few suggestions, which surprised me. Who knew other people would be worried about the same thing. But then I thought about all the weird shit people said they believed and somehow it didn't seem so strange. It suggested a few things, one of which was to use apps that use algorithms to scramble your brain waves making them harder to read. It also suggested head gear and meditation.

"Might as well try an app," I said and found one to download.

"Go ahead and start on these booklets and I'll work on the flyers," Dad said as the two of us settled into work and getting through two large orders. "Any plans for today?"

I sorted through the supplies I'd need and checked the proof for quality before setting up the print. "I'm going to meet Cole in Hickory Crossing later." I tried not to smile when I said it but lasted all of zero seconds.

"Do you two have plans once you get there?" he asked while he was busy setting up his own print job.

"There's a lady there that saw him get hit by the lightning, we want to talk to her about it." I didn't tell him everything this time, it had gotten too strange, and I didn't want to worry him or make him think I was losing my shit.

"I didn't realize you two were still working on that," he said and glanced at me.

"Yeah. Cole wants to know what she saw. besides what she already told him. He's doing great, and nothing new has come up, but I think he's just curious."

"Well, I'm glad you're going with him. I doubt he remembers too much. I hope he's able to find out what he needs to put it all to rest."

"It's been weighing heavily on him. It's not like it's something that happens every day." That part was true. Cole was very focused on the event, and I didn't think he'd ever be able to completely put it to rest until he had more answers. Especially after he found out about that guy Nox.

"I'm glad you were there to help him," Dad said again, and I wondered what he would think if I told him it seemed Cole now had the ability to read minds. "Bobby?"

"Oh, sorry, I was daydreaming."

He huffed a laugh at me and went back to working on the pamphlets he'd started, and I hoped the time passed fast, because I wanted to know what Miss Avery could tell us too.

TWENTY

Cole

SINCE BRIAN WAS BACK and feeling better, things were mostly back to normal. I could focus on customers and restocking while he took care of the receipts and the schedule. Since basketball season was ending and baseball season would soon begin, the store was busy with parents and students buying new shoes and workout clothes.

My mind had been mostly silent so far today, and I hoped that continued. I had just helped one young man who was playing on the baseball team for the first time, so I wanted to make sure he had everything he needed to play and be confident. He was more than a few inches taller than me and obviously athletic, so I hoped he had enough talent to have a great first season.

"Thanks, Cole, you've been very helpful," his dad said as I rang them up and packed everything into a bag.

"You're welcome, and good luck this season," I said as I handed it across the counter to them just as the bell at the door sounded. There stood Bobby. He slid his sunglasses off and gave me the sexiest grin as he stepped around the family that were just leaving and walked closer to me.

"Hey," he said, before leaning in and kissing my cheek. My eyes met Brian's where he was at the back of the store fitting someone for hiking boots. He smiled before shaking his head and getting back to the boots. "Are you almost done?"

"Yes, I just need to clock out." I turned back to the computer I'd used to check out the last customer and clocked out. After waving to Brian, we walked out of the store.

"How was wor—" Bobby started to say before I pulled him in for a kiss.

"Sorry, but I've been thinking about you all day."

"Don't you ever apologize for kissing me," he said and rested his hand on my hip.

"You're all I've thought about since last night." I wasn't the type to chase another guy, but everything felt different with Bobby.

"What time are we supposed to meet her?" Bobby asked.

"Now." I laughed after checking the time. "Come on, let's go see what we can find out from Miss Avery. Oh, her name is Anna. I guess I still call her the same thing I did as a kid."

"Anna, got it. Did you want me to drive?"

"Actually, why don't you follow me to my house then I don't have to leave my car here," I said, and the two of us walked to our vehicles. His was parked out front so he waited while I pulled out from the back parking lot, and he stayed right behind me until we pulled up in front of my house. He hadn't been here since the day we met, and I hoped this time Mom didn't stop by unannounced again.

"Is it okay to park here?" he asked, and once I nodded, he turned off his engine.

"Let's go in my car," I said, and he moved over to the passenger door. As soon as he was in the seat, he leaned over and kissed me again.

"Just checking that it felt as good as it did earlier," he said and grinned before pulling his seat belt on. "Are we ready?"

In that moment, I could have thought of at least a hundred things we could do together that didn't involve going to talk to Miss Avery. "Not yet," I managed to say before leaning in for another kiss. For a while we sat in front of my house and made out like teenagers. Not me when I was a teenager. But the popular kids who had no trouble flaunting themselves in front of the kids who had no chance of meeting someone in this fucking town. Kids like me.

Bobby took my face in his hands and met my eyes. His thoughts were a swirl of emotions, and I opened my mind to see if I could read his thoughts. But there was a heaviness that made it hard for me to focus. "We should probably go, I don't want to keep Anna Avery waiting," he said.

"You're right let's go. Do you have to work tomorrow?" I asked and put the car in gear.

"Nope, I have tomorrow off."

"Funny thing, so do I," I said and turned to find him staring at me.

"Maybe we can go to dinner or something when we're done."

"Or maybe we can order pizza and watch a movie at my house," I replied as I drove out of town toward the small goat farm owned by Anna Avery.

"What movies do you like?" he asked.

"I'll watch anything, but I love action, science fiction, paranormal, comedies. Like I said, pretty much anything."

"Well now I'm intrigued. How about if I choose the first movie, and you choose the second," Bobby said, and in his thoughts, I sensed amusement but nothing clear. The whispering was quiet today and I was thankful.

Hearing Bobby say was he wasn't in a hurry to go home was music to my ears. "I love that idea. Now I'll have to think about what to choose."

For a few minutes neither of us spoke as we drove along the same road I'd jogged on that morning. I'd avoided it since then and stuck to either jogging around town or at the track of the high school. It wasn't the same as being out in the middle of nowhere, but it worked for now.

"Right there is where you got hit," Bobby said, and pointed out the exact spot as I slowed down. I could still see the charred spot on the road and a rush of emotions hit me. I wasn't sure if it was my own or Bobby's, but I needed to pull off the road. There was a narrow gravel strip that I swerved onto and took a deep breath when the car lunged to a stop.

I could hear Bobby talking to me, but I couldn't understand what he was saying. There was so much going on in my head: static, a rush of wind, sirens, and noises I couldn't identify, then softly at first, it started.

With a flash of blue—

The words were whispered, and they were all I could hear over the tempest of noise screaming in my brain. I grimaced in pain as Bobby leaned over to me but all I could focus on were the words getting louder and louder in my head. "Stop!" I screamed.

"Cole!" Bobby shouted. That broke me out of whatever was happening. It was like snapping awake after falling asleep at the wrong time in the wrong place. I was instantly alert and aware of him near me. "What happened?" His eyes were mad with worry as he smoothed my hair back from my face before pulling me into an awkward hug. Everything stopped then.

"There was a lot of noise in my head, but mostly the voice was there again." He leaned in to look at me closer before cupping my cheek.

"We don't have to go speak to Miss Avery today," he whispered.

"We *have* to. This might be the only chance we have to warn her."

Twenty-One

Bobby

"This was a bad idea, we should never have come here," I said as I watched Cole grimace in pain fighting whatever invisible battle he was fighting.

"We need to go to her," he said, and put the car in Drive.

"Cole, be careful," I pleaded and was thankful we were on a country road with zero traffic. He turned off onto the narrow dirt lane that led to the house I'd noticed the goats at before. As soon as we pulled up, the door to the house swung open, and the lady I'd noticed that day walked out on the porch.

"Cole Ryan, you need to get in this house right now," she said, and glanced around her property as she spoke. Never once sparing me a glance.

"Anna, you're in danger," Cole said as he got out of the car and walked around to my side. "I need you with me." He reached out his hand and I opened the door and took it.

"He knows you have the power he wanted. Nox won't stop until he gets it," Anna said. She was maybe in her late sixties, but she didn't look like some weak little old lady, not at all. "Get inside."

The two of us rushed inside and she slammed the door. "Miss Avery, we came to tell you about Nox," Cole said.

"I already know. Listen." She watched Cole and waited a few seconds before speaking again. "Haven't you noticed that your mind has quieted now you're here?" she asked, staring hard at Cole.

He closed his eyes and concentrated. He took a deep breath and relaxed, but then his eyes shot wide open. "I can't hear the other noise and voices in my head. There're only my thoughts now. But how?"

"This house has many protections. My sister also practiced magic, but not the way Nox did. She met someone and left him with me. I've never seen her again. He was fond of telling people she died in some horrible accident but that wasn't true." Anna walked over to the couch and sat down. The house was small but neat with lots of pictures of her when she was younger and sepia-colored pictures of relatives from long ago.

"You're the guy in the van that helped Cole when he was struck." She stared straight at me, not looking away or blinking. Her eyes were a clear blue. Her weathered skin and nearly white hair made her eyes even more intense.

"Yes, I saw it all happen and I drove him to the hospital." I didn't really know what more to say. I didn't want to reveal anything that Cole didn't want her to know so I stayed quiet.

"My mom told me about Nox, and the summer they spent together with my dad," Cole said, and took a seat close to Anna.

"The power you now possess was what Nox had been after for as long as I can remember. He always wanted to be able to read minds, but I never really took it seriously until he got older. He killed one of my goats as a sacrifice to something. I didn't care what his reasons were, I made sure it couldn't happen again."

"What do you mean?" Cole said, as I tried not to think about some guy I didn't know, making one of the goats a sacrifice.

"There used to be an old lady that lived near here. She knew a lot about magic. I didn't know anything about that stuff. I knew farming and was more than happy to live my life out here doing just that. One day she showed up here when Nox was still quite young. She told me that he could be influenced by dark forces if he chose the wrong path. She also told me how to ward the house against any power." She pointed out small markings that were on every door frame and even along the baseboards. "He can't tell what we're talking about when we're inside, and he can't read your mind."

"He can read my mind?" Cole asked.

"Yes, and he can connect with your consciousness and suggest you do things you would never in a million years think you'd do," Anna said.

"I've heard his voice in my head. But he always says the same thing over and over. Before we went to the carnival, his voice was the only one I could hear. But as soon as we crossed the entrance something changed. But Bobby seems to calm the storm in my head."

"With a flash of blue," Anna said.

"What does it mean?" I asked and squeezed Cole's hand.

She drew her lips in a tight line and took a deep breath before she answered. "Nox was killed in one of his many attempts at power. The voice you're hearing is all that's left of him. He didn't want my body or just anyone else's, he wants someone who can hold the very power he wanted, and that person is you, Cole."

"What are you saying?" I asked, barely able to get the words out.

"With a flash of blue there will be two—that means you and Nox. Both of you could wield the power of the blue lightning. There's far more to it than just reading minds." She looked at both of us. "One of old and one of new. Nox would be your parents' age now, and you're new to this power. Wisdom and innocence must combine, if one of them is to remain alive. He wants to inhabit your body, and he does have the knowledge of magic to do it."

"What?" I all but shouted. "How could this happen?"

"If Cole isn't strong enough to resist then Nox will take over. He's already in your mind. You've felt him, haven't you?" She gave Cole a critical look and I waited for him to say she was wrong. But instead, he turned and looked at me.

"Remember at the hospital the voice that was speaking wasn't me? I didn't understand it then. I was aware of it, but I knew for a fact it wasn't me. I think that was him. It was a bit like standing back and watching someone else control me."

"What about at the carnival?" I asked.

"The carnival in Woodland?" Anna asked.

"Yes, we went there for a date. As soon as we crossed the entrance, I could hear everyone's thoughts all at once. Almost like a switch had been flipped."

"Or a veil lifted," Anna said.

"What do you mean?" I asked.

"Nox wouldn't want you to be able to use the power that he thinks is only for him. He'll hide it from you at any cost. But something about that carnival must have revealed it while you were there. Can you still hear thoughts?"

"Not everyone. Some I can without any effort while others I can read an emotion but not thoughts."

"Imagine if you could read every thought as someone had it. What would you do with that information? Would you use it for good or bad?" Anna said.

"I never wanted this power, and for sure I never wanted to be hit by lightning. This whole ordeal has been horrible. I don't want to know what anyone is thinking."

Anna smiled then. "Cole, I've known you nearly your whole life. But I still needed to make sure you were not interested in using this power for your own gain. I will help you to break the connection Nox's spirit has with you. But it won't be easy." She turned then to face me. "You, I don't know at all. But not many would help a stranger the way you did, and it's obvious you care deeply for Cole. Hopefully your connection is strong because you're going to need it."

"I've never felt as connected to anyone as I do to Bobby."

"I hope that's true, but either way we'll know soon enough."

TWENTY-TWO

Cole

ANNA EXPLAINED EVERYTHING SHE knew about Nox and what she thought his powers were limited to. "Right now, he's not as much of a threat. I don't believe he's even a spirit, more like his energy is all that's left, but if he can shove you out and take your body, there's nothing that can stop him. No barrier will hold him."

"How can he just be energy?" Bobby asked.

"It has to do with the spells and rituals he was using. He didn't care if he survived them, only that there was enough of him left to carry on in another form. His obsession with power took over his life and destroyed him." Anna stared off, lost in thought about who knew what.

"What do we do? I didn't know anything about the mind reading until the other night. And honestly, I prefer not having that ability," I said, and took Bobby's hand. "I don't want to know what everyone is thinking. But it hasn't been nearly as intense as it was those first moments. Maybe he was wrong, and I don't even have the ability? Or it's fading."

Anna turned her gaze on me again, and I tried not to look away from her. "Carnivals are unique places. Some are just what they appear to be, while others are places where true magic can be found. Maybe the one you went to had a stronger magic than Nox and when you entered, his magic was stripped away."

"Can that happen?" I asked, making Bobby laugh.

"After everything we've seen the past few weeks, this is not the strangest idea we've heard. Tell her about how it changes when we're together," Bobby said.

"I guess there's nothing I can't believe now. Bigfoot, the Easter Bunny, everything is real," I said, and Bobby laughed again.

Anna smiled. "You two just met the day you were in-jured?"

"Yeah, I was on my way to town to make a delivery and Cole was out jogging. I hadn't been to Hickory Crossing before that," Bobby said.

"Almost like something intervened to make sure you were both at the same place at the right time," Anna said.

"Do you really think that's possible? I mean don't get me wrong. But you know how it is around here, nothing ever happens, and just the fact he was driving down your road at the same time I was jogging along it seems like just a strange coincidence."

"I'm not sure. Although I don't know what role you would play in all this," she said to Bobby.

"When we're close he can quiet my thoughts. But only when we're close. It feels like he's able to help me repel the voices." I tried to explain something that had no explana-tion. I hoped it made sense.

"That may come in handy if Nox tries to hurt you when you two are together, but you need to find more ways to protect your thoughts and yourself. He'll be probing your mind for information to use against you. Things you're afraid of, things you've done that you don't want to think about. He may even haunt you in your dreams."

"He's started coming to me in my dreams. I haven't had any dreams that I knew were him, but there's been a heaviness when I fall asleep. Like I know something is just out of sight and if I let my guard down it might be the last time," I said, and I knew Bobby wouldn't like that I hadn't told him. I turned to him. "I didn't want to scare you. There's nothing you can do to protect me when I'm asleep. Anna's right, I need to find more ways to protect myself."

"I put an app on my phone that's supposed to mess with brain waves and make it harder for you to read my thoughts," Bobby said, and his face tinted pink. "I was desperate, and I wanted to see if it stopped you from reading my mind." He shrugged and grimaced.

"Did it work?" Anna asked.

"He couldn't read my thoughts on the way here, but I wasn't sure if it was because of the app or other reasons," Bobby said and glanced at me.

"I don't know if something like that would work, but right now I'd say you should try everything you can. You also might want to find someone connected to the other side that can give you some protection. I can help a little, but Nox will be doing all he can to make sure you lose. You'll want to do all you can to protect yourself." She took my hands in hers and looked me right in the eye. "There won't be a second chance, Cole. Once you're lost there won't be a way to come back."

"I don't have any idea where I'd find someone like that. This is all new to me," I said. My throat was dry, and I sort of wanted to throw up, but at the same time I knew it was time for me to step up and take control of my destiny and not allow anyone or anything else decide for me.

"We'll figure it out," Bobby said. "I'm sure there are people who can help. I'll do whatever I can." The sincerity in his voice didn't surprise me, but it did worry me. I didn't want to put him in danger simply by association.

"Bobby, this isn't your fight. You're stuck in this because of me, and I care too much about you to let you risk yourself."

"I didn't ask your permission. I told you I'd help, and I meant it. I'm more than capable of making my own decisions." He was angry, and I understood that feeling. I took the choice away from him and that made him fight it even more.

"Bobby, I couldn't live with myself if you were hurt. I just want to keep you safe." He stood and paced across the small living room. His fists tightened and flexed as he tried to control his emotions. Finally, he moved back over to me.

"It's my choice. My choice," he said and pointed at his chest.

His eyes met mine and were filled with too many emotions to sort through, so I pulled him into my arms instead. "I'm sorry," I whispered.

"It's my choice, and I choose you. I won't leave you vulnerable."

He was so brave and deserved far more respect than I'd given him. Everything in me told me to trust him but I hated the idea of him being hurt in any way. I needed him, and I decided that maybe together we had a better chance of both of us getting through this. "Thank you," I said, before kissing him hard. "I really do need you."

TWENTY-THREE

Bobby

"IS THERE ANYTHING ELSE you can tell us?" Cole asked Anna.

"No. I had no idea he was willing to do something like this or that he had the ability or the power. But there is something else I want to show you." She stood and walked down the hall to one of the doors. "Over here."

Cole and I stood and walked to where she stood with her hand on the knob. "This was his room. I haven't changed anything," she said before opening the door.

I sucked in a shocked breath as the three of us walked in. Every wall was painted in a mural. It started on one wall with the road out front of the house, then on another wall was a man on the road. On closer inspection I would have sworn it was Cole. The next wall was bolt after bolt of blue lightning hitting the man and him being knocked backward. The last photo was another man standing over the one on the ground, but it wasn't me. "Who is that?" I pointed at the figure who stood holding his arms above his head. His dark hair covered his face, but I knew he wasn't anyone I'd met.

"That's Nox," Anna said.

"So, this is a mural of him giving Cole the power, then taking it away?"

"I believe so," Anna said, and walked closer to the last picture. There was no furniture in the room, only a small desk that was covered with piles of notebooks and bottles and jars of different things. None of which looked familiar.

I opened one of the notebooks, but it was blank. "Did he write down anything?" I asked.

"Not that I've found. I doubt he would have written down what he did or how he did it. I don't even know how he started learning to do the rituals he was doing or when it took a turn to the dark powers. If he was following directions or just coming up with things off the top of his head, I just don't know." She scanned the room, and her hard exterior gave way to a vulnerability; I saw her as an aunt who had lost a nephew to something she didn't understand.

I opened another notebook, and this one was full of writing, but all of it was line after line with the same five words. *With a flash of blue.* "Look at this," I said, and showed the two of them.

"This might sound harsh, but did Nox have mental illness?"

Anna thought about Cole's question before answering while I walked around the room and looked at the painting more closely. What I had thought was dark paint outlining the bolts of lightning was actually very small meticulous writing. "Did you notice this?" I asked, before Anna could answer Cole.

Both of them leaned closer to the wall. "What is it?" Cole asked.

"If I had to guess I'd say it's the spell he used to call the blue lightning," Anna said. "See this?" Her work hardened hands traced a passage that I would have missed. All of it was written so small as it followed the outline of the light-ning, making it hard to read if you didn't pay attention.

"This is a spell?" I asked.

"I have learned that it's not so much which words you use, but how you use them. I think this was his plan. It looks like it details all the steps he took to make it all happen. But it's not in any order that I can see," Anna said as she leaned over to get a better look. "This isn't the same as the poem, this is all the steps he took." She pointed to one part that was low on the wall. "This is where he started making sacrifices to any dark power that was willing to help him."

"Do you mind if I take some photos of this?" I asked.

"Bobby, I want you to do whatever you can to help Cole. I don't want either of you to get hurt over what my nephew did. I'd also recommend you put some protection in your own houses. Nox won't stop. If he's started reaching out to Cole in his sleep, it's probably just the beginning."

I took a few pictures and tried to get as much of the writing as I could. It was interwoven into the image and not easy to see, but once I knew what I was looking for it was easier. "It looks like it starts at the bottom and the more he wrote the higher up the wall he wrote it."

"Why would he write it all down?" Cole asked.

"Probably for proof that he actually did it," Anna said. "Anything he did that had to do with dark magic, he made sure someone knew. I think that's why he involved your parents. He knew they were not involved in the dark arts, but he wanted to show them what he could do. His ego may have also contributed to his demise. To answer your question about mental illness, as far as I know it had nothing to do with that. He had a genus IQ and instead of using it in a positive way, he decided to do all he could to obtain a power that he obviously could not control."

"We'll find out all we can. Are you safe here?" Cole asked.

Anna smiled at him. "I'm fine. There's nothing he can do to me that he hasn't already tried. Plus, he can't affect my thoughts. I'm not sure why but he was never able to use any influence over me. I keep the house warded so he knows he's not welcome here, but even if his energy could enter the house, he could not touch me."

"You're sure?" I asked.

"Yes. You two need to worry about yourselves. Especially you, Cole. He won't stop trying to get that power from you. No matter what the cost for either of you. He was obsessed when he was alive, and now that he's not I think that obsession is all that remains. He won't stop, Cole. Not until he's taken over your body or destroyed all that's left of himself."

"I'll be careful," Cole said.

"I wasn't kidding when I said you should put some protection on your house." She picked up one of the notebooks and scribbled a few images into it while we watched. "Use these. Put them near doors and windows. They'll keep your thoughts safe and keep him out of your space. Remember, he can only get to you if you let him. He doesn't have a physical form and that does weaken him in some ways, but it makes him stronger in others."

"Thank you, and we'll let you know what we find out from the mural," I said. The two of us walked back out to the door.

"Good luck, boys," Anna said, and as soon as we were on the porch she closed the door behind us.

We got back into the car, and before we left, I noticed her looking at us through the window. Her demeanor was completely different than what we'd seen when we were inside. If I had to guess, she looked terrified.

"Let's go back to my house and see if we can figure out more about the mural," Cole said and started the engine.

Twenty-Four

Cole

I DIDN'T FEEL ANYTHING when we left the house, and I hoped that meant Nox was staying out of my head. It was horrible to imagine he'd been in my head, but it was even worse to imagine what he could do if I didn't fight him.

"What did you think of all that?" Bobby asked.

"I'm not sure. None of this makes any sense. Like the carnival, how could going there strip away the power Nox had been using on me? I just don't know enough about this world to know what to think."

"Me either. I really do think we need to find someone who does know. Let me see what I can find out this week," Bobby said. "Don't worry, Cole, you're not in this alone. I promise I'll be there for you." He reached across and took my hand and pulled it over to his leg. "We'll figure it out."

"I hope you're right. I keep thinking I can ignore it and it'll go away. But like today when Nox was in my head, it comes out of nowhere and there's no warning. I feel like he's got the advantage, and all I can do is try to be prepared for whatever he does next."

"When we get to your house let's see if we can copy all the writing into one document. It would be easier to read if it's all laid out for us," Bobby said.

Neither of us spoke as we drove along the country lane back to my house. When I pulled up out front to park neither of us moved. Bobby's thumb glided across the back of my hand, and I closed my eyes and focused on the feel of it. I really liked Bobby, but I didn't want him to get hurt, and if he continued to be with me, eventually he would.

"I know what you're thinking, and I'm not leaving. We're in this together until the end," Bobby said, and turned to face me.

"I couldn't live with myself if you were hurt in any way, Bobby," I whispered, unable to choke out the words that would tell him to leave.

"Let's go inside." Bobby kissed my cheek before opening his door. "You're not getting rid of me that easy." He smiled as he waited at the front of the car for me.

"I don't want to get rid of you. Far from it." The more time I spent with him the more I was drawn to him. It felt deeper than any attraction I'd ever felt, and that scared me. I'd been in a few relationships but none of them were that serious, and none of them left me feeling helpless with worry about the other person.

I unlocked the door and as soon as we were inside, I pulled him into my arms and kissed him. "I don't want to get rid of you. The way I feel about you scares me but excites me at the same time. I've never met someone like you," I confessed. All of it was true, and there was something in the air that made me frantic to tell him, but I wasn't sure what that was.

He kissed me again before slowing it down and resting his forehead against mine. "No more talk of me not helping. If it gets too intense or I don't feel safe, I'll remove myself from the situation. But until we know exactly what we're dealing with I can't make that decision."

"Okay. I'm just so confused about everything. And just when I think we've figured something out it all changes. I'm not used to so much chaos and uncertainty." I looked deep in his eyes as I spoke. I needed him to know I meant every word. "You're more important to me than anyone has ever been."

"Really?" he murmured, before kissing me again leaving me breathless. "I think I could kiss you forever."

"I want you," I whispered. Tired of thinking of everything else and ignoring the burning desire I had for him.

"Then have me," he said surprising me. He kissed me again and walked me backward until my knees hit the couch and followed me down without breaking contact. He was about to lie down on me when he jumped up and hurried to the door. "Just in case your mum stops by." He turned the lock and slipped his shirt off as he slinked back to me.

I didn't know if he worked out, but his body was toned and fit, and my fingers itched for a touch. He reached for my hand and settled it on his chest with his hand covering mine before leaning in for another kiss. "Now you," he said, and tugged at my shirt.

His hands were on my chest as soon as my shirt was out of the way, squeezing my pecs before finally leaning in and licking my nipple. My hips thrust off the couch, and when his eyes met mine this time, they were filled with fire. He still hadn't lay down on top of me and I wanted that press of his weight, but when he settled his hands on the waistband of my jeans and slipped his fingers inside, I couldn't nod my head yes fast enough.

He eased my pants down and I was so hard my dick slapped back onto my stomach. Before I could even open my mouth to speak, he knelt at the side of the couch and sucked me down. A grunt escaped me that surprised even me, but I was too lost in sensation to care. My hand shot out and I gripped his hair and tried not to let my body take control no matter how fucking good it felt.

"Oh g—" He stopped me with a hand on my lips.

"My name is Bobby, it's the only name I want on your lips when you're about to blow." I nodded and tried to encourage him to slip out of his jeans. When at last we were both naked, I pulled him onto the couch so we could both pleasure each other at the same time. His dick was thick and hard, and I didn't waste any time swallowing him down as much as I could manage. We were on our sides at opposite ends of the couch, both of us in a battle over giving the other pleasure while taking the time to enjoy it.

I gripped his ass and pulled him closer as I buried my face in his pubes and breathed him in. He smelled fresh and clean, and I wondered what body wash he used because I never wanted to forget it. His hands smoothed down my leg and back up to where his fingers slipped into the crack of my ass. Just knowing how close he was to my hole made it that much hotter and made me want him that much more.

He lifted my leg and slung it over his shoulder and pulled me in even deeper while gripping my balls and slipping a finger just behind them. I wanted to groan, but I also wanted to shoot so bad my eyes rolled back in my head. Bobby knew exactly what he was doing and a few more strokes from his tongue, and I was done. My body thrashed and jumped as he swallowed me down and reached down to his own straining dick. He squeezed himself and I had regained just enough control to move his hand away and double my efforts. In just a few seconds he followed me. My mouth was flooded with his taste, and it made me want more.

He sat up long enough to turn around and face me. "You're amazing," he said before kissing me again.

Twenty-Five

Bobby

I HADN'T MEANT TO take our relationship to the next step, but with Cole I felt like every moment was precious and needed to be embraced when the moment presented itself, and it had when we arrived at his house. Once we'd cleaned up and gotten dressed again, the two of us sat next to each other on his couch. He had his laptop on his knees while I tried to figure out what the words were that were written all through the mural.

"None of this really makes sense," Cole said as he typed out what I read and entered it into a document. "It's all incoherent ramblings."

"Hopefully in all the ramblings we find something we can use. Just one clue as to how to get him out of your head."

"Do you really think the drawings Anna gave us can help protect the house?" Cole asked.

"I'm not sure, but I think she probably knows more than either of us. It can't hurt to try," I said, and was so tempted to move in for another kiss. But not yet, we had work to do.

"You're right, and it's not going to hurt anything to try it." I opened the notebook Anna had drawn the symbols in and the two of us took a few minutes to copy them here and there around his house. I put one above the door small enough to not be noticed but I made sure it was exactly like Anna had drawn it. Even if there was nothing to these symbols, it made me feel better knowing they were there.

Afterward, we sat a while longer writing down the mishmash of words and phrases from the mural. "Want to get a pizza?" I asked when I realized we'd been here a few hours.

"Yes, and I could use a break. Want to watch a movie?" Cole asked and took out his phone. "What do you like on your pizza?"

"Anything," I said and closed my phone from where we'd been looking at the images from earlier.

"Are you staying tonight?" he asked and glanced at me from the corner of his eye while still looking at his phone.

"Are you asking?" I smiled and leaned a little closer.

"Yes, I'm not ready for you to leave," he said, his honesty hitting me right in the feels.

"Good, because I'm not ready to leave either." We put the laptop and notebook away and got comfortable on his couch before choosing a movie. It was all very normal, and for a while I forgot we were in the middle of a paranormal crisis that could cost Cole his life.

"How about a beer?" he asked.

"Sure, I could go for a beer." He walked into the kitchen and as he was rummaging around in the refrigerator, there was a knock at the door. "I've got it."

"Here you go," a guy with a pizza restaurant hat said, before he shoved the pizza and a bag at me and jogged back to his car.

"Thank you," I yelled at him as he drove away. I walked in just as Cole was setting two beers on the table in front of the couch.

"Perfect timing," he said and took the pizza and everything else from me and set it on the table too. "Now let's see how this movie is."

We settled in and ate pizza while watching a terrible movie that we both laughed at and actually enjoyed. It was all normal. And I knew it wouldn't last.

We went to bed early, both of us ready to relax and have a little quiet time. Sleeping naked in his arms was comfort beyond belief. He held me close, and I tried to control my body and enjoy the cuddle time. Cole fell asleep and the soothing sounds of his deep breaths lulled me to sleep.

"I will have him," Cole said, waking me up. Turning to look at him, I could see in the dim light of the room that he was asleep. I smiled, thinking he was talking in his sleep.

"It doesn't matter what you do. He will be mine and I will claim the power that was meant for me," Cole said, but it wasn't Cole. And he wasn't talking in his sleep. "You know this to be true. I've seen your thoughts and how you worry that he's lost to me. Well, your concerns are true. He will never be yours because he's already mine."

"I won't let that happen," I said through gritted teeth.

"There isn't anything you can do to stop it," he said.

"You're wrong," I sneered and leaned up on my elbow.

"Bobby?" Cole said, his voice full of sleep and his eyes barely cracked open.

"Cole?" I said and leaned in closer to look.

"Is something wrong?" he asked, suddenly wide-awake.

"Everything is fine, I think I had a bad dream," I lied.

He pulled me close and kissed the top of my head. "I'll protect you, go back to sleep." He was asleep almost instantly while I lay there awake hoping I could keep him safe.

Twenty-Six

Cole

I woke up with Bobby covering most of my body with his own. His head tucked into my shoulder and his arm slung across my stomach with his leg draped over both of mine. Closing my eyes I hoped for a little more time like this. Just to feel the warmth and safety of his touch, but I knew eventually he'd wake up and it would be over.

He drew in a deep breath and kissed my chest. "Good morning," he whispered.

"Good morning," I said and wrapped my arms around him, holding him right where he was. "I could wake up like this every morning."

"I bet you wouldn't say that in the summer when it's hot and sticky." He slid far enough away to rest his head on his hand while keeping his leg slung over me.

"I'd probably try to ignore that I was dying of heat," I said, making him laugh.

"What are your plans for the day?" Bobby asked.

"I want to write down more of the mural. I doubt we find anything in it all, but I'd like to make sure." He nodded before leaning in for a kiss.

"Why don't we go out to breakfast and relax before starting that. I can help you for a while but then I need to get home."

I tried to remember the last time I went to breakfast with someone who wasn't a family member and sadly, I couldn't remember anything recent. "That sounds great." The thought of spending a little more time with Bobby away from the usual madness that followed us was more than inviting.

"Cole?" Mom yelled from the front door. Bobby's eyes widened in what I would have sworn was fright before he scrambled for a blanket to cover himself.

"Back here, do not come—" was all I got out before she opened the door.

"There you are. Good morning, Bobby," she said to the lump where he was completely covered up. "I just wanted to know if you were coming by for dinner later."

My family sometimes got together for Sunday dinner. It wasn't anything planned and sometimes it was just one or two of us, but it was a tradition from when I was a kid and when I had time I went. "I'm not sure. We're going out to breakfast then I have a few things to work on today."

"Okay, well stop by if you get hungry, we're eating at six. Your sister has requested lasagna. I haven't decided if I'll make one or cook a frozen one." She spoke to me, but her eyes were locked on Bobby, who still hadn't moved at all since she'd walked in the room. "You're welcome too, Bobby."

"Thank you," he said from underneath the covers.

She grinned at me, obviously enjoying the fact she was making Bobby so uncomfortable. I rolled my eyes at her which she returned. "Bye, boys," she said as she walked out the door.

"It's safe," I whispered. He slowly poked his head out and looked around the room before flinging himself on top of me and kissing me.

"Let's go eat," he said after another big smack. We were both dressed and out the door in less than thirty minutes and once again it was all just so nice.

The sun was shining, it was a beautiful clear day, and I don't think I'd taken the time to enjoy a morning in months. Bobby took my hand and pulled me to his car. "I'm driving," he said, before holding the door open for me.

"What a gentleman," I said, making him laugh.

He hurried around to the driver's side while I slid into my seat and buckled up. "Where to?" he asked when he got in and started the car.

I gave him directions to a small local restaurant that had a covered garden and was aptly named Garden of Eden. "This looks nice," he said when we walked in.

"Morning, Cole, just the two of you?" Janine, the owner, asked as soon as we walked in.

"Yes, and can we eat outside?" I asked.

"Of course," she said and led us out there. It was a beautiful space, and once again, normal. It was busy, but not so busy that we felt rushed or that other patrons would be waiting for a table if we took time to enjoy it. So, we did.

We talked about anything and everything, and I was reminded how much I really liked Bobby even though I didn't know him all that well. He was interesting, and funny, and truly a really nice person. I found myself waiting for his accent to slip through, and when it did, I couldn't stop myself from smiling. "What are your plans for the rest of the day?" I asked just as our food arrived.

"Not much. I do need to do laundry and get ready for the week. But nothing set in stone. Are you going to your parents' for dinner?" Bobby asked.

"Probably. Then I don't have to worry about cooking for myself."

"Do you cook?" Bobby asked.

"If you count opening a can or putting something in the microwave as cooking. I mean I try, but it doesn't always work out."

Bobby laughed at that and the two of us were quiet for a few moments while we ate breakfast. It was funny how even when we were quiet there wasn't any sense of needing to speak. I was happy just to be in his company, and I hoped he felt the same. "How's your food?" I asked.

"So good. This was a great choice. We'll have to come back here again," he said.

"I'd like that," I said, and I hoped through all the weird shit, the two of us could have one more day that was fucking normal, but somehow in the back of my mind I knew that would be a hard-won battle. But in this moment, I was willing to fight as hard as I needed to for Bobby and me. Because he was worth it, and nothing was going to make me give up on him. I hoped he felt the same, because I knew at some point, we'd both need to choose to either stay and fight or ignore everything we'd seen and go on with our lives.

TWENTY-SEVEN

Bobby

I STAYED A SHORT time longer at Cole's house before deciding it was time to go home. I pulled Cole into my arms and held him while we swayed back and forth, just inside the door to his house. "I had a nice time, thanks for asking me over."

"I did too, and I'm going to miss you in my bed tonight," Cole said.

"I'll miss you too, but if I don't go now, I probably won't leave." He smiled at that and kissed me one last time before opening the door for me.

"Bye, Cole," I said and waved as I hurried to my car. He stood outside as I drove away, and I wished I could have stayed but there was something else on my mind that I didn't want to share with him. We needed every chance we had to get rid of Nox and the only place I could think of that might have some answers was the carnival we'd gone to.

The more I thought about it the stranger it seemed that he'd suddenly been able to hear thoughts when we'd gone there, but also that after talking to the guy from the entrance, he'd been able to shut it down, so he wasn't in pain. I also wanted to know if it was possible Nox was hiding the ability to read minds so Cole wouldn't know he had that power at his disposal.

The exit for the carnival came up fast and I was relieved to see it was still there. I exited the freeway and drove the short distance down the small country road that led to the large open field that was being used as a parking lot.

I parked close to the entrance and sat in my car a moment after turning off the engine. The place was a mess of activity as some workmen walked around cleaning up, while others were hurrying to food stands with supplies or fixing anything that needed to be repaired. It looked so different during the day, and if I didn't know better, I'd have sworn it was a throwback to the old carnivals from long before I was born. And who knew, maybe it had been around that long.

A workman walked by carrying a garbage bag and I hurried out of my car. "Excuse me, would you know if the men that were working at the entrance on Friday are here today?"

He adjusted the bag and walked closer to me. "Ah that'd be Errante and Rafe. You can find them over by the big tent." He pointed to the largest tent in the carnival, and after thanking him I hurried in that direction taking the same route we'd walked Friday. There at the end of the row was the large tent. All the sides were pulled up allowing me to see inside. I could see a few workers gathered around in the tent talking quietly as I got closer.

"Excuse me, can I be of some assistance?" one of the men from the entrance asked as I stepped inside the tent.

"Yes, I'd like to speak to you and the other man who were working the entrance on Friday."

"Is there a problem?" the other man said. He was dressed like a ringmaster, and I wondered how I hadn't noticed that the other night. Both of them were mesmerizing in their beauty, so I blamed my lack of attention on being distracted.

"No, no problem. I came here the other night with my friend Cole Ryan. He had an odd experience while he was here, and I wanted to speak to you to see if this had happened before." A look passed between them for a split second before they both turned to me.

"I'm Errante Ame, and this is my ringmaster, Rafe. I remember you, but I'm not sure I remember who your friend is." They waited while I pulled up pictures of Cole and hoped one of them recognized him.

"Oh yes, I do remember him. He appeared to be having a panic attack near the food booths," Errante said.

"It wasn't a panic attack. I know this will sound strange, but Cole was hit by lighting a few weeks ago. Since then, he's had many strange things happen. As soon as he crossed through the entrance to the carnival, he was able to hear everyone's thoughts." I waited for their reaction, not really sure what they'd think of some random stranger walking into their show asking about something as unbelievable as hearing thoughts.

Rafe murmured something close to Errante's ear and turned back to me. "I have some matters to take care of before the carnival opens. Good day, and good luck to you," he said before walking out of the tent.

"Are you quite positive your friend can read minds? That sounds a bit far-fetched," Errante said, bringing my attention back to him.

"No more far-fetched than a carnival that looks like something from days gone by suddenly showing up near where we both live," I said, and hoped to get some reaction from him.

"What is it you want from us?" Errante asked, completely ignoring my comment.

"We spoke to someone else who has a connection to all of this, and she thought that maybe, when we walked into the carnival, it stripped away a power that might have been hiding the fact he gained the ability to read minds when he was struck by lightning."

His eyes grew intense and somehow darker as he stood there silently. "The carnival is many things to many people. Anything is possible here, and if your friend was meant to know he had contracted some such ability, then it is possible he could have been shown that truth when he crossed the entrance. But he would not have gained any such abilities while he was here. We are just a carnival no matter how we appear to you."

"I'm sorry, I didn't come here to accuse you of anything, it's just we can't seem to find out any real answers. Everything we know is either someone else's opinion or rumor." I clutched at my hair as I realized there wasn't any big revelation found here either.

"If your friend has been touched by magic, that magic would leave a trace. A psychic may be able to help him figure out exactly what happened and learn how to control his abilities. But I'm afraid there isn't much else I can do to help." He looked concerned but I also couldn't shake the feeling there was more to this carnival than just a roadside attraction that moved town to town.

"My mum used to go to a psychic in Dublin that she swore told her when she'd get pregnant and the exact date I'd be born. But I don't think she's gone there for a few years."

"We have a fortune teller here, if you and your friend would like to stop by the carnival after we open, you're welcome to have an audience with her," Errante said.

"I think I'll ask my mum about her friend first. If she can't help us, then we'll come back."

"Very well. I'm sorry I couldn't offer more assistance."

"It's okay, you actually helped. I hadn't considered speaking to a psychic. Thank you, and I'm sorry if I was rude before," I said before shaking his hand and walking back the way I'd come. I hurried back out to my car. As soon as I closed the door, I was on the phone to my mum.

"Hello, Bobby, what are you up to this weekend?" she asked. Being from Dublin, my mum still had a heavy Irish accent that I would always equate with making me feel safe and content.

"Hi, Ma. I've been to Hickory Crossing with Cole. Mum, I think I need your help."

"What is it, son?" Her voice was full of concern, and I was more thankful than ever for her compassion and willingness to always help.

"This is going to sound strange, but remember the psychic you used to talk to years ago?"

"You mean Saorise?"

"Yes, do you still speak to her?"

"I do, but not as often as I once did. Since we moved here, I only speak with her on the phone or if we do a virtual session."

"Do you think she'd be willing to have a session with Cole and me?" I hoped she said yes because I wasn't sure who else we could find that could possibly help. I shook my head at blowing the chance to ask the fortune teller at the carnival to help. But something told me this was the way to go.

"She's always willing to help, Bobby. Let me call her and see what she says."

"Thanks, Ma, I've been freaking out about how to find someone to get us some answers. I'm really worried about Cole."

"I want you to tell me everything," she said. So, while I drove back home, I did. Dad was a great listener, but Mum was a believer. She never once doubted anything I told her, from the weird blue lightning to the fact that Cole could now read minds. When I finished it felt like a weight had been lifted.

"Rest easy, son, I'll see what I can find out."

I hung up just as I pulled up to my house, and for once I felt what might be the beginnings of hope.

TWENTY-EIGHT

Cole

THE SUN WAS JUST beginning to set when Bobby called. I put away the laptop and pictures we'd printed earlier and answered his call. "Did you make it home?"

"Yes, I just pulled up to my house. Do you miss me yet?"

"I do miss you," I said, and tried to ignore the way my cheeks hurt from smiling so wide.

"So, I wanted to talk to you about a few things," Bobby said, his voice suddenly serious.

"What's going on?" I hoped he wasn't about to tell me he was done with all the weird shit, but hell, even I was done with it. I just wanted more normal boring days like today.

"I stopped at the carnival on the way home," he said.

"What for?"

"I wanted to see if I could find out more about why you could hear thoughts once we were there."

"I hadn't thought of that. What did you find out?" I asked and held my breath waiting for his reply.

"I spoke to the two men that were at the entrance. I didn't get the feeling they were open to telling me too much, but one guy, Errante, gave me an idea. He said if you had been touched by magic it would leave a trace, and a psychic might be able to help you learn more about it."

"I don't know anything about that," I said, and cold dread washed over me. First it was lightning, then hearing other people's thoughts, now magic and psychics? What was next, werewolves and vampires?

"I spoke to my mum. I don't know if I told you, but she's gone to a psychic for as long as I've been alive. In fact, one of them told her when she'd get pregnant and when she'd give birth. I know it sounds crazy, but I can tell you it's the real deal." Bobby was serious and I trusted him no matter how crazy I might have thought this was a few months ago.

Now I knew there was a whole world out there I knew nothing about, but that didn't make it any less real.

"Where is this psychic?" I asked, not sure what else to say.

"She's in Ireland, but my mum does sessions with her virtually, so she's going to ask her when she's available and whenever that is I'm going to make sure we're both there. I won't let you deal with this alone." The sincerity in his voice rang out clear and my heart clenched at the thought he cared enough to make sure he was there for me. That meant more to me than I thought it would.

"Let me know and I'll make it happen. I know the time difference might be an issue so just tell me and I'll come to your house. I mean if that's okay with you." I didn't want him to think I expected an invitation, but I knew I'd be a nervous wreck if I was home by myself and I knew he was in the middle of it by himself. I'd never talked to a psychic before, and I would have been lying if I said I wasn't nervous. But if it helped me to be rid of this power and all the bullshit surrounding it, I was more than willing to try anything.

"I'll let you know. I really think it's better for you to come here. My mum can join us, she has a lot of experience with psychics, so she'll know just what to ask. I hope you don't mind, I filled her in on all that's happened."

"Bobby, thank you. You didn't have to do any of this, and I want you to know I really do appreciate it. If I was on my own—well I'm not sure what I'd do," I said, and swallowed the lump that had formed in my throat.

"We'll figure it all out, and we'll get through this," Bobby said, and I believed him. Because Bobby wasn't a quitter and he'd done everything in his power to make sure I was safe and that we had as much information as we could find. "I mean it, Cole."

"I know you do. I just worry what happens next. Every time we find out one thing, it seems like something else happens. I can't live my life always waiting for whatever weird thing comes next."

"I wish I was there to hold you. Please don't give up hope. I promise, Cole, we're going to figure it out."

"Thank you, Bobby." His words touched a part of me I never knew existed. The part of me that wanted love and needed to know there was someone out there who would care if I wasn't here anymore.

"Did you find anything in the mural?" Bobby asked, thankfully changing the subject.

"I did find one thing, but I'm not sure what it is exactly or if it means anything."

"What is it?" he asked.

"I was working on that one part that was written smaller than the other writing. There was a word I didn't recognize. Haniel, any idea what that means?" I shuffled the paper I'd printed off to make it easier for me to keep track of what we'd gone over already and what was still left.

"No, it's not familiar to me. Did you try searching?" Bobby asked, and I knew he'd be on it when he put the phone on speaker.

"No, I just found it before you called. It was all written so small I had to blow it up and print it off. It's more of the same ramblings but then that word, over and over again." I typed the word into the laptop and scrolled through the results. "That can't be right."

"What did you find?" Bobby asked, but I could tell he was seeing the same thing.

"An archangel," I whispered.

TWENTY-NINE

Bobby

"I've spoken to her, and she's very concerned about what all this means. Saorise says there has been rumblings through the psychic plane about a man who has been trying to gain a power that is too strong for him to wield. They had not known who that person was or how he was going to try to gain the ability, but they knew it had to do with reading thoughts and being able to control a person once he was in their mind," Mum said as she rushed through my door, her long blonde hair pulled back in a braid, her green eyes flashing with worry and intensity.

"Is she able to speak to Cole? Wait, did you say control a person?" I thought back to being in the car when Cole had to pull off the road.

"Yes, she was very concerned. But she has an understanding of those things that I cannot even comprehend so it's just best you speak to her. She'll be available tomorrow at six. It'll be the middle of the night for her, but she said she'll make sure she's there. Bobby, she also said to avoid any places where there is strong magic, it could have unforeseen consequences," Mum said.

"The carnival," I murmured.

"Yes, but you didn't know. So, from now on be careful until we figure this all out," she said.

"You'll be there too when we speak to her?" I asked, and she pulled me in for a hug.

"Of course I will." She was worried, and while I was happy not to be stumbling around without a clue, I also didn't like the idea of my mother being at risk from powers we didn't understand. "Don't worry, I have many protections. Whoever is behind this won't be able to influence me."

I let out a deep breath and squeezed her tight before releasing her. "What does Dad really think of all this?"

"He doesn't understand the magic part of the world, but as you know he'll support us in any way he can. He's a good man and he'll stand strong with us no matter what."

"I need to make sure Cole is safe. I'm not sure why but I feel very protective of him."

"It may be that the fates made sure you were there to protect him, or it could be that seeing him injured in that way bonded you to him but either way I understand, and I'll do whatever I can to help you both."

"Thank you. I feel like we've been so alone in this other than the woman in Hickory Crossing that saw Cole when he was struck."

"Who is this woman?" she asked, her brow furrowed with concern.

"Anna Avery, she's the aunt of the man that put everything in motion. She said her nephew had been trying to gain power for years, and she thinks he's the reason Cole was struck. But she also thinks he wasn't trying to give Cole the power, she thinks he wants to take over Cole's body."

"Where is her nephew?" Mum asked.

"She said she lost contact with him years ago and thinks he's dead and all that's left of him now is energy. That's why he wants to take Cole."

"Son, it's a very difficult thing to put one consciousness into another body. Are you sure he's dead?"

"I just trusted what she said. Cole knows her but I'd never seen her before the day he was struck. I noticed her standing in her field watching when it happened." Listening to myself say it all out loud, my mind swirled with worry and confusion.

"Please tell me you have not gone to her home," she said.

"Yes, we went there the other day. She told Cole she had information on her nephew and showed us his room." I took out my phone and showed her the photos I'd taken and the marks that were scattered throughout her house. "What's wrong?" I asked as she recoiled back from the photos and covered her mouth with her hand.

"Those markings are not protection. We need to find out exactly who this person is," Mum said. She looked at the mural and zoomed in on the picture to see the writing. "This is spellwork. If it wasn't her, then whoever painted this was using this drawing to bring this scene into reality."

"Cole called me before you came in and said he'd found a strange word in the writing, Haniel. I looked it up, it's one of the archangels. Do you think Cole is in danger?" A cold chill ran down my spine. I hadn't considered Cole was in any danger at home. I mean he worked at a sporting goods store in a small town in the middle of nowhere, how much trouble could he get into?

Mum thought about it before she answered, but when her eyes met mine, I knew she was still worried. "It depends on who this other person is and what they want. If they are indeed magical and they have a plan they've set in motion, then we'll need to find out what that plan involves. Saorise is a very talented psychic, but she's not magical and there is a limit to what she can do. But she should be able to give us a better understanding. I'm not knowledgeable about archangels but I do know most of them are very powerful and not all of them have good intentions."

Worry consumed me and it took everything in me not to drive right over to Cole and stay with him just to make myself feel like I could keep him safe. But I knew it didn't matter. Neither of us were safe from anything that was either magical or paranormal. We had no clue about it and didn't know how to protect ourselves or to keep it away. *The symbols.* "Anna told us those symbols would keep Cole's home safe." I thought about how we'd both put those symbols all over his house.

"Show me them again," Mum said. She squinted her eyes as she looked closely at the pictures I'd taken of some of the symbols that we'd used at Cole's. "This symbol here is to give an opening for spirits to contact you, this one is to call them. She's done the opposite of protection. She's put a bullseye on Cole." Her eyes were wide with fright and for a moment neither of us moved, but then her phone rang, making us both jump. "It's Saorise."

"Answer it," I said.

"Yes, I understand," she said while her eyes were locked with mine. "I'll make sure. Thank you, I know Bobby will appreciate it." She hung up and took both my hands in hers. "She said tomorrow around six is best. But in the meantime, to cleanse this area and reinforce it so nothing can come in that's attached to Cole."

"Is he going to be okay?" I asked, and hoped she really did know what she was doing.

"We're going to do all we can for him," she said while I hoped like hell that was enough.

THIRTY

Cole

After Bobby's call I was lost in thought about everything he'd told me. It was all strange and a world I wasn't accustomed to. I'd found the name of the archangel in the writings but when I searched it up, I also found that archangel was associated with psychic abilities and enlightenment. I didn't want psychic abilities, and I really didn't want other people's thoughts in my mind. I glanced at one of the symbols we'd placed around my house, and I hoped they worked to keep Nox or whatever it was, away from me.

I tried to keep busy with laundry and chores, but my mind was still on Bobby. I missed him, every time we were together, I couldn't wait for the next time I'd see him. I hadn't gone to my parents' for dinner, and I regretted it since it would have kept my mind off Bobby. I tried to keep busy, so I didn't keep looking at the phone, but the busier I was the more I worried I'd miss his call. I was about to call him when my phone rang.

"Hey, I was about to call you," I said.

"Miss me already?" he asked, but his tone was different than it normally was.

"Yes, more than you know. Is the psychic able to meet with us?" I asked, not wanting to press him too hard but needing to know.

"She can meet with us tomorrow at six. She said she'll stay up for us and that is the best time. Are you able to make that?"

"Yes. Give me directions to your house and I'll make it happen. Is there anything I need to bring?" I asked, not sure at all how this worked.

"You're going to think this sounds weird, but you'll need to be cleansed before you enter. Mum is going to cleanse my house and make sure nothing that's attached to you can enter here." He was silent and I imagined him sitting there waiting for my reply.

"I don't know how any of that works," I admitted.

"Me either, but my mum knows enough for both of us. I never mentioned it before, because I never thought it mattered. I didn't tie the two things together."

"What do you mean, Bobby?"

He took a deep breath and released it before speaking. "My mum was once part of a group of people who were all talented in different mystical ways. She doesn't have psychic abilities, but her friend Saorise does. She's a very strong psychic."

"What do you mean mystical?"

"More than I can explain on the phone. I don't even understand it all. I know that archangel is probably involved, but I don't know how. Then there's the fact my mom thinks Anna is the one pulling the strings, not Nox." He was rambling and I tried to keep up but it was confusing and some of it just felt wrong. "I'm worried for you. Mum said the symbols Anna gave you for protection do not protect, they do the opposite. It's all I can do not to drive back to you right now."

"Should I remove the symbols?" I glanced around the room expecting to see something strange.

"I don't think you should mess with any of it. We've probably done enough, and I don't want to take the chance of doing something else. Please just stay safe until tomorrow."

"I'm not going anywhere. I'll stay home and drive right to your house after work tomorrow," I said and glanced around again. "I don't feel good keeping those symbols up. I think I'd feel better if I just clean them off."

"Okay, and I'm so sorry we didn't know this before."

"I don't expect you to know this stuff. We're both doing the best we can. I'm going to go now, but I'll be there as soon as I can tomorrow."

"Take care, Cole," Bobby whispered.

"I will, you too." I hung up and immediately got to work scrubbing away the symbols we'd scattered all over the place. Thankfully we'd both worked in each room at the same time and my house wasn't exactly big, so it wasn't hard for me to find them. As I wiped the last one away the whispering started. Low at first then just loud enough to make me listen. But it wasn't the voice I'd heard before.

I concentrated this time and tried to figure out what it was saying.

I can't forget to get up early and go meet Gloria at the gym. No matter how tired I am I need to make myself go this time.

The words became clearer the more I concentrated on them, even if I had no clue what they meant. But then I remembered. The neighbor had recently joined a gym. I'd seen her leaving at the same time I left for work, and I knew she didn't start work until later. Could it be I really was reading her thoughts?

Thirty-One

Bobby

I regretted not insisting Cole come here as soon as I hung up. Now it was sometime after four and I was still tossing around in my bed unable to sleep. Every time I nodded off visions of Cole being struck by lightning invaded my dreams. Only in most of them he didn't live, and he was either blown apart or burned alive. Finally, when the sun had barely begun to rise, I gave up and got out of bed.

There was no way I'd be able to sit at home, and I knew there was plenty of work at the print shop, so after a quick shower I got dressed and drove the short distance. Dad was already there as usual. It didn't matter how early I arrived, he was always there first.

"Morning, Bobby, you're here early," Dad said when I walked in.

"I couldn't sleep so I thought a little work would do me some good," I said, making him laugh.

"Well, there's always something to be done here." He set me up with a job that would take most of the day. Booklets that were fully printed and then I'd need to bind them all together. A few hours had passed, and I'd finished around half of the interior pages.

"Could you use some help?" a familiar voice said from behind me.

"Cole?" I asked, because I couldn't believe he was here. I pulled him into my arms and finally felt like my world wasn't going to shake apart. "I'm so happy to see you."

"I didn't sleep at all last night. There was no way I could work, and I knew if I sat at home, I'd be a mess by the time I could go to your place. I hope you don't mind—" He was a rambling mess; his eyes were bloodshot, and his hands shook as he wrapped his arms around me.

"Son, why don't you take your friend home. I think you both could use a little sleep," Dad said from where he stood by the print machine he was using. "I've got this, you go on now."

I took Cole's hand and led him over to where Dad was adding more paper to the machine. "Are you sure? I don't mind staying. Cole can hang out until we're done."

"I'm sure, you two go ahead." He smiled before starting to turn back to the machine.

"Dad, this is Cole Ryan. Cole, this is my dad Keith Sanders," I said, and the two of them shook hands.

"Nice to meet you. Bobby's told me about how you met. Are you doing okay since you were injured?" Dad patted Cole on the shoulder, and I knew he was probably as worried as I was.

"Nice to meet you, Keith. I'm sorry to meet you under these conditions but I didn't sleep at all last night."

"Now, don't you even worry about it. You two go to Bobby's and get some rest. Don't worry, I'll put you to work on a day when you're feeling up to it." Dad grinned and winked at me.

"Thanks, Dad. I'll make it up to you, I promise." He waved to us both and I helped Cole back out to where we were both parked.

"How did you find me?" I asked as I poured him into my car.

"I remembered the name of your business from the van. I googled." He smiled at me as I slid into the driver's side. "I'm sorry to just show up, but I couldn't sit at home waiting for something else to happen."

"You were on my mind all night. I couldn't stop worrying about you," I said, and kissed him. He looked up at me and even through his exhaustion I could see it. Fear. He was afraid, and I was almost too scared to ask why, but we were in this together and I knew he needed me.

"What happened?" I whispered.

"I cleaned up all the symbols. At first it was a relief. It creeped me out seeing them all over my house, and when you said they were not meant for protection I didn't see a reason to keep them there. As soon as I removed the last one, the whispering started. Only it wasn't the voice I'd been hearing. I'm pretty sure it was my neighbor. All night I could hear them in their dreams, everyone who was nearby, and some that were not so close. But I realized I can control it. I can push them down to where I can think over them." His eyes closed and I could imagine him just falling asleep right there.

"You didn't hear Nox?" I asked, almost afraid to know.

He shook his head. "I really need to sleep."

"Let's go then." I started the engine and made the short drive to my house. He'd fallen asleep so fast I was afraid he wouldn't want to wake up, but as soon as I turned off the engine, he jumped. "Sorry, we're at my house."

"Thanks, Bobby." The two of us got out of my car and I helped him to the front door.

"I'm amazed you could drive here."

"There were a few times I wasn't sure I could make it, but I made myself keep driving. I needed to be with you." I helped him inside, and right to my room. As soon as I eased him down on the edge of the bed he slid over to his side.

"Let me take your shoes off at least," I said and slid them off. He immediately pulled his legs up and patted the bed behind him. After stripping down to my briefs, I slipped behind him and pulled him close. Both of us took a deep breath and slept.

Thirty-Two

Bobby

"Bobby." My mum's voice was right next to me as she shook my shoulder. "It's almost time."

"What?" My eyes shot open, and I sat up. She stood there with her arms crossed, staring at Cole who was still asleep.

"I don't suppose you somehow cleansed him before you brought him home?" she asked.

"No, I didn't—wait, what do you mean?" I was still blurry eyed when I remembered she'd told me to not let him enter without cleansing. My eyes shot open, and I jumped out of bed. "Sorry, Mum, I—"

"Go take a shower and wake up. I'm going to cleanse the house and Cole," she said, and gave me a good push when I walked past her.

I did as she said without even thinking. I turned on the shower and after stripping off my briefs, I stepped in before it was even warm. The cold water woke me up faster than a shot of caffeine would have, and within a few minutes I walked back into the bedroom.

Cole was still asleep curled on his side, but Mum was walking around the room fanning sage smoke all over the place including Cole. I walked to my dresser and after getting some clean clothes, I slipped them on as she made her way into the rest of the house.

"Sorry, Ma, we were both so tired all we could think of was sleeping."

"It's okay, it doesn't seem to have done any harm. I don't sense he brought anything in with him. We got lucky," Mum said as she continued to spread the scented smoke around the house. When she finished, she walked over to me with a jar of coarse salt and instructed me to spread a thick line of it in front of both doors to the house.

"What about the windows?" I asked.

"Only the doors," she said. "Go wake up Cole when you're done."

I did as she asked and spread a thick layer of salt in front of both doors and walked back to the bedroom. Cole was sitting on the edge of the bed and looked relieved when he saw me. "Hey, sorry to leave you, Mum put me to work."

He stepped over to me and once again pulled me close. "It's okay. I want to do whatever she thinks will help."

"I need the two of you out here," she called from the living room. I took his hand and led him out to where she stood. "Cole, I'm Bobby's mum, you can call me Sara. I'm going to need to cleanse you again and make sure nothing can reach you while you're here."

"I'm willing to do whatever it takes. I feel like I should tell you what happened last night." While she once again wafted smoke around him, he told her what he'd told me earlier about removing the symbols from his house.

"And you didn't feel like someone else was in your head?" she asked but seemed skeptical.

"Not this time. It was just me, but I could focus on the voices and hear what they were saying. It was so different, as though it was a natural thing and I knew what to do," Cole said as she finished.

"Can you hear our thoughts?" Mum asked him.

He closed his eyes and took a deep breath. "Bobby's worried the salt won't stop something if it wants to come in." His brows drew together as he concentrated harder. "I can't hear your thoughts. It's like I know they're there, but I can't reach them." He opened his eyes and looked at the two of us. "Was I right?" he asked me.

"Yes, and I'm really glad that's all I was thinking." Cole smiled at me, and I knew he wasn't listening to my thoughts anymore.

"If you'd have been able to read mine, I'd have worried. You see, while I don't have magic, I do have an ability, but it's defensive. I can block out anyone or anything that would try to not only enter my mind, but any type of spell or power that would try to control me against my will." She glanced at me then and shrugged her shoulder. "You didn't need to know."

I could only stare at her wide-eyed. There was no point in arguing about it, she was right. It didn't concern me. "Okay then. Are we ready for your friend?" I asked.

"We still have a few minutes, but we might as well set up the laptop and gather anything we might need. I'm talking about a few candles, the sage, and even the salt." Cole helped with the table and chairs while I turned on the laptop and made sure it was connected and ready to go. Mum set the candles and other supplies nearby before drawing a circle of salt around where we'd be sitting. "Just in case," she said.

The three of us sat at the table and after logging in I clicked on the link Saorise had emailed me. It only took a moment for the site to connect and her screen to come to life. On the small screen was a woman I'd seen before. She was my mother's age with long curly red hair and skin so pale it must have never been touched by the sun. She had a smattering of freckles across her nose and a warm smile.

"Well, what do you say we get on wit it?" she said in the heavy Irish accent that reminded me of my home.

"Hello, Saorise, we're all ready here," Mom said.

"Good to know, Sara, now let's begin. I imagine you must be Cole?" she asked and looked right at him.

"Yes, ma'am," he said.

"There be no need for formality here, Saorise will do." She smiled then and her warmth bled through the screen.

This was the woman I recognized as my mother's friend. "Cole, I'm going to ask you a few questions then I want you to take hold of Sara's and Bobby's hands. They're going to be my connection tonight. Would that be okay with you?"

"Yes."

"Do you come to me willingly?" she asked.

"Yes, I do."

"Do you come to me with an open mind and a willingness to be rid of any evil that may be lurking nearby you?"

"Yes."

"Very well then, take their hands." The three of us linked our hands on top of the table and immediately Saorise's head dropped backward.

"You have been chosen," she said.

"For what?" I asked before anyone else could.

"The Tuatha Dé Danann has chosen you to be the one who will be enlightened."

"That can't be right," Mum said, and tugged on my hand. "Saorise, that isn't right."

Saorise's eyes opened then but gone was the deep brown and instead her eyes were now a pale white. "It is as it shall be. Haniel has chosen him."

"What does she mean?" I asked while Cole still sat with his eyes shut.

"The Tuatha Dé Danann are what the ancient celts called angels. But it can't be real."

"It can and it is," Cole said at the same time Saorise did. "I was chosen, and it is as it shall be."

"Cole?" I said and leaned closer to him.

"He will be enlightened," Saorise said just as Cole started to glow with the same blue as the lightning.

THIRTY-THREE

Cole

I COULD FEEL THE power of the lightning course through my body, but this time was different. It was a slow warming feeling and not painful or terrifying. If anything I felt a calm wash over me, and my mind was opened. I knew that Saorise was good and had no ill intention in using her abilities to help people. The same with Sara. Her ability was indeed defensive, but she never used it to hide anything or protect herself unless she needed to. They didn't need to tell me, I knew everything about them now.

Then there was Bobby. I could feel his hand in mine, but it felt far different than Sara's. His touch filled me with strength, and—love. He gave me hope and helped me to see not everything was bad. We were meant for each other, and it was going to happen even if we fought it. We were supposed to meet that day on the road, and he was meant to save me.

He was my light in the dark, and my protector. In my imagination I saw him glowing with the same blue light of the lightning. He didn't know it, but he had power too; he wouldn't know about it or need it for a while. It would be there when he called it to him.

As I sat with my eyes closed, my mind raced with images and information that seemed endless. Familiar faces and complete strangers all flashed through my mind, but now I knew everything about each of them. Even if I had never heard their thoughts, I knew them, and they knew they could trust me. The two were connected. I would be the guardian of their thoughts, and they would trust me to help them when they needed me. And I *would* help.

"Cole, the time has come for you to know all," a voice said from the edge of my consciousness. It wasn't a voice I'd

heard before and I wasn't sure if it was male or female, but I could feel power emanating from every word.

"Why me?" I asked, finally able to form a coherent thought of my own.

"It matters not why you were chosen, only that you were. Many events have put this in motion, and now the time has come for it to be so. Dark magic was used to try to force me to endow my gift to someone who was not worthy. It almost worked, but fate put you there, and the lightning chose you instead."

"Anna?" I asked.

"The one you know as Anna is not who she pretends to be. There have been many times through the years we have stood back and watched as they tried to take power that was not meant for them, but each time, we were able to avert it. This time they tried to draw that power directly from me, and it almost worked, but your presence stopped it. Do not think they will not try to take this ability from you. It is what they hold most dear and won't give up without a fight."

"What do I do?" I asked.

"There is only one way to put things as they should be," the voice said, and spelled out everything I'd need to do. Somehow, I knew exactly how I'd do it, and I knew without a

doubt it would work. As the voice spoke, I could see it all play out in my mind, and I knew no matter how difficult the task might be, I could do it. *We* could do it because Bobby was there too, and he was just as important as I was.

"Bobby?" I said, and squeezed his hand to remind me he was there.

"Cole, I'm here."

"Haniel has shown me what will happen. There's no avoiding it, we can only be ready."

"What do you mean?" Bobby asked as I opened my eyes. When he met eyes he gasped, and I knew he was shocked to see my eyes now glowed the electric blue of the lightning. I leaned my head on his shoulder drawn to his warmth and comfort.

"Soon, you'll understand. But for now, just know nothing that has happened was a coincidence, or chance. Everything was meant to be."

"Now you see," Saorise said with a critical look and soft smile.

"Yes, thank you for helping me."

"You'll need to be ready. The one who would take your power knows you have accepted it. As we speak, they prepare to try to take it from you. It won't be easy to stop them. They have lived many lifetimes and changed forms many times to gain the considerable power they possess."

"I know, but Haniel has shown me the way."

"Your future has shifted and my vision of it is not as clear as it was. But I know you yourself can see your future, and you can also make it what you want it to be," Saorise said. "As Sara has said we're part of a group that shares our powers and use them to help when needed, we'd be honored to have you join us. We can all help each other."

"I'd like that. Even though I now have the knowledge, I'll still need guidance. This is too much power for one person to decide how to use it." I squeezed Bobby's hand, and he squeezed back. "Bobby would also need to be included." He had no clue what was ahead for him, or us. But he was strong and smart, and both would serve him well.

"I don't have anything to contribute," Bobby said.

"You have more than you realize. Soon you'll see. You're more than an equal to Cole. You two are strong alone, but together you're like a shield and sword. An unbreakable power that will bring the darkness to heel."

Sara looked at Bobby with a look of both awe and pride. "I don't know how I didn't see it before. Bobby, they're right, you do have power."

"He's your son, are you really that surprised?" Saorise said, making us all laugh.

"Well, you didn't say his ability was stubbornness," Sara said with a chuckle.

"You'll both need guidance, I hope you know you can come to us anytime you need advice," Saorise said. "You have been given a great gift, but you'll need to learn to control it as well as use it wisely. If we're done here. I'd really like to get to bed."

"Of course, thank you so much. I can't tell you how much I appreciate you taking the time to meet with us," I said, and after Sara and Bobby both said goodbye, Bobby ended the session.

"Do you feel better?" Sara asked us. I still hadn't let go of Bobby's hand and didn't intend to.

"Yes, it's all clear now," I said, and Bobby gave me an odd look. I knew he didn't understand, but he would.

THIRTY-FOUR

Bobby

I DIDN'T UNDERSTAND EVERYTHING that had happened, and I knew Cole had somehow gotten information the rest of us were unaware of. But he was so calm now, and I felt myself pulled to him even more than I had before.

After we cleaned up all the salt and Mum left, the two of us stood in my kitchen with our hands held between us in silence. "It's going to be okay," Cole said.

His words soothed me, and I knew on a deeper level than I'd ever felt that every word he said was true, and I could always trust him. I leaned in to kiss him, and the heat between us grew and swirled around us in a building storm of passion and fire. "Stay tonight," I whispered.

"As if I'd want to be anywhere else," he said before kissing me again. We stumbled through the house to my bed where we fell onto it while stripping pieces of clothing away. When we were both naked and pressed together, I again had that sense of how right it was with us.

"I don't think I've ever wanted anyone as bad as I want you," I said. I wasn't someone who was overly sentimental or felt the need to express every feeling I felt, but that was also different with Cole. I thought I might be falling in love with him, and I struggled to imagine him not being in my life.

"I feel the same way," he said, and I wasn't sure if he'd heard my thoughts about my feelings for him, but right then I didn't care. "I need you."

He guided me between his legs, and I realized he wanted me to fuck him. I was worried. This single moment meant so much to me, and I wanted to get it right. Opening the drawer to my dresser I took out the lube and condoms and set them on the bed next to him. I sat up and settled my hands on his chest. "Are you sure?"

"Surer than I've been about anything in a long time," he said. I leaned in and kissed him. Our tongues swirled together, and my dick got harder. I reached for him to find him just as hard and swallowed his gasp when I touched him.

After squirting some lube on my hands, I pumped him firm and slow with one hand while fingering him with the other. When I knew he was so on the edge that he'd be done in one more stroke, I stopped and tried to open the condom. The package slipped and slid in my fingers as I struggled to rip it open. Finally, he lay his hand over mine.

"Let me help." He smiled up at me, but the fire in his eyes had not dimmed and his dick was still just as hard. Our breaths were loud in the quiet room as he opened the packet and slid the condom on me with a stroke. He then guided me to his hole while I slowly pressed into him. He grunted when I was all the way in and squirmed around to adjust.

"Oh my god," I breathed out. He was beautiful and everything I never knew I needed. And it felt like we'd known each other far longer than the few weeks we had. I slowly started to move and slung his leg over my shoulder. We kissed and I would have sworn we were connected on a spiritual level. The press of his lips against mine, his tongue searching for mine as we kissed like our lives depended on it. I wasn't sure how I'd ever survive without him being right beside me.

I pulled him up on top of me as I leaned back and let him take control. He rode me with zero hesitation and didn't slow down one bit. Our kisses got sloppier and sloppier as both of us chased an end that neither of us were going to give up easily. I lifted his hips just enough to pound into him, and he threw his head back. He looked like a god, his abs flexing as he held himself above me and his hands clenched on my legs as he let me give him every bit of his pleasure. His head was thrown back while his mouth opened to gasps of pleasure.

Finally, I couldn't take it anymore and reached for him. After two pumps he came and when his ass clenched my dick, I followed. One of his hands rested on my chest as we fought to slow down our breathing. I slipped out of him and after tying the condom and tossing it in the trash, I wet a washcloth with warm water in the bathroom and walked back over to where he still hadn't moved.

"That was amazing," I said as I kissed both of his closed eyes, making him smile. After cleaning up I wrapped him in my arms, and this time it was me keeping him safe just like I hoped I always did.

"You're amazing," he mumbled and scooted back closer to me. "Thank you for tonight."

"What do you mean?"

"This morning, I was confused and terrified of what could happen to me. But now I know exactly what's coming and we'll be ready. They won't be able to beat the two of us."

Once again, I wasn't sure exactly what he was talking about, but his voice held so much conviction and confidence I found I wanted to believe every word he said. "I'll do anything I need to. Just tell me whatever you need."

"When the time comes, you'll know what to do," he said just before he drifted off to sleep.

"I hope you're right." After that I fell asleep and slept better than I had in months. It was as though all the worry and dread were lifted, and nothing was left but warmth and happiness.

Thirty-Five

Cole

Last night had brought many answers and with it many questions. But thankfully more answers and a deeper connection to Bobby than I would have ever expected. He was so much more than he imagined himself to be. And soon he'd know, he was meant for more than working at a print shop. Not that his job wasn't worthy, it was, but fate had other plans for him. For us.

I woke up early and sat on the edge of the bed. A twinge reminded me of last night, making me smile. "Hey, do you need to get going?" he asked and kissed my shoulder.

"Yes, I don't want to leave them stranded again. I mean not like there could be a huge rush, but you never know," I said, making Bobby laugh.

"I'm going to shower then I'll buy you a coffee for the road."

I watched as he walked to the bathroom and just before he was about to close the door, I said, "A man after my own heart." The smile he gave me said a lot and I rolled over to check my phone as he started his shower.

There were a few emails and some texts, mostly from my boss making sure I'd be there today, which I answered first. I liked my job and Brian, my boss, was also my friend, so I didn't want him to worry that I wasn't going to be there. There was also a phone call from a number I didn't recognize and a voicemail. I dialed it and listened when someone answered.

"You won't win. It doesn't matter that you have the sight. The power will still be mine." The voice was strange, and I didn't recognize it, but I knew without a doubt it was Anna.

"We have already won. There's nothing you can do now," I said and kept my voice calm even though deep inside I wanted to scream at her to leave us the hell alone.

"We'll see about that." The phone went dead just as Bobby walked out of the bathroom wearing nothing but a towel. I tossed my phone on the bed and moved to Bobby, needing his warmth, and wanting to hold him in my arms one more time while we were still skin to skin.

"Everything okay?" he asked and kissed my head.

"Yes, everything is just like it's supposed to be. Brian sent me a text, so I need to get going. I don't want him to think I'm flaking on him, and I still need to go home, shower, and change."

"I can give you some clothes to wear if you want to shower here," he said.

"That actually sounds nice." I kissed him before walking past him to the bathroom. "I won't be long."

While I was in the shower, I thought about all that had happened the past two days, and how much better I felt about everything. But then I remembered the thoughts I'd been shown, things that were to come of which I had no control over. I knew it was all necessary, but it would be emotionally, as well as physically, hard. But in the end, it would all be worth it. I'd also been shown that, and I couldn't wait until it was all over.

I walked out of the bathroom and found everything I needed on Bobby's neatly made bed. I heard him in the other room and hurried to put on the clothes he'd given me.

"Hey, it looks like everything fits," he said and handed me a piece of toast.

"Thank you, and yes it's not a bad match." I took a bite and realized we hadn't eaten at all yesterday. "I might need to stop and get something more to eat on the way home."

"We must have been tired if we forgot to eat, but don't worry. There's a place near work that serves breakfast. We can go there if you want. It won't take long."

"That sounds great," I said, and once again was amazed how normal this all was as we walked to his car. "Your house is nice. I don't think I mentioned that before. I like it out here." It was peaceful and quiet where he lived just outside of town on a small plot of land next to where his parents had their larger house. For a moment I just listened. The sound of birds singing and the breeze through the trees were all I could hear. No traffic or people. Just nature waking up.

"Thanks, I enjoy it here. It's much quieter than Dublin. We lived in a boisterous neighborhood that were all huge football fans. You would not believe how crazy it would get for every match." Bobby shook his head as we got into his car.

"Do you miss living there?"

"Nah, it's nice here. I wouldn't mind going back for a visit, but this is my home now." He backed out of his parking spot and reached for my hand as he pulled onto the main road.

"I'd like to see Ireland sometime."

"Then we'll make it happen. I'd love to take you around," he said as easily as he'd offered me his clothes earlier.

He drove us to the small restaurant he'd mentioned that was really more like a to-go counter. We both ordered strong coffee and something to eat. Once I started eating, I made short work of the breakfast sandwich I'd ordered, and as I took the last bite, I noticed Bobby had finished his too. "Okay, let's get you to your car so you can get to work," he said.

It only took a few minutes, and we were there, and I hated that we wouldn't be able to be together today. "How late do you work today?" he asked.

"I'm done at five. What time are you done?"

"I have a print job to finish, but I have a delivery that's near Hickory Crossing, would you mind if I stopped by your house later?" He parked his car and glanced over at me. I lunged at him and kissed him hard.

"Yes, I mean no, I don't mind. Please stop by," I said, and kissed him again making him laugh.

"I will. Now you'd better go, or I won't want to let you leave," he said, and took my face in his hands to kiss me. He held me so gently and poured so much emotion into that kiss, even though I forced myself not to read his thoughts I could feel his emotions, and his love.

THIRTY-SIX

Bobby

"WELL, YOU LOOK A lot better today than you did yesterday," Dad said as soon as I walked in. "Sara said everything will be better now." Dad didn't try to delve into all the things Mum did, but he was always supportive, and she shared just enough to not keep any secrets from him.

"Yes, it's amazing what a good night's sleep will do." I went over to where I'd left off yesterday, and after just a few hours I was nearly done. "I noticed we had some deliveries to make, mind if I do them?"

"I was hoping you would. I know there's a delivery near Hickory Crossing. Maybe you can go see Cole," he said like he needed to talk me into it, but I was ready to go there after work anyway if it didn't work out.

"Oh yeah, I don't mind at all," I said and tried to hide how happy that made me.

"Well good thing you don't mind. The other deliveries should be on the way if you plan it out right." The two of us packaged all the deliveries which would nearly fill the van.

"I didn't realize we had so much." I used a handcart to carry a few loads of boxes out and once it was loaded, I walked back in to make sure I had it all.

"You're good to go. Guess I'll see you tomorrow," Dad said.

I rubbed the back of my head and forced myself to stand there until he walked back into the shop. I was strung tight, and I couldn't wait to leave but he saw right through me and waved me off. "See you tomorrow," I said as I climbed in the van.

It had taken longer to complete delivering the orders than I hoped. But a few minutes before Cole would be done for the day, I drove into the city limits of Hickory Crossing and right up to the sporting goods store. It had only been a few hours since I'd seen him, but it felt like it had been days. For a moment I sat in the van and looked through the big front window of the store he worked in.

Inside I could see him helping someone find a fishing pole and I smiled as I watched him go over everything with the young girl who stood next to an older man. Cole was patient and listened as they asked questions and never made it seem like he was in a hurry or didn't have time for them. His eyes met mine through the window and we both smiled. This guy turned me inside out without even trying and before I knew what I was doing I was opening the door to the store.

"Hey, I'll be right with you," he said as he walked the two customers over to the cash register.

"I'll be here," I said and tried to look busy. I'd just picked up something in the fishing department that I had no clue about when warm arms wrapped around me from behind.

"Can I help you," he said into my ear.

"I hope so, I was really missing you and was hoping you were almost done with work." I tried to sound cute but made myself cringe, making him laugh.

"Go on, Cole. You'll be useless the rest of the day," a man I knew was his boss yelled from behind the cash register. "I'll see you in the morning."

"Let's get out of here," Cole said and after clocking out, he grabbed my hand and dragged me outside. "I'm so happy you're here."

"Me too, want me to follow you to your house?" I asked, not sure where we'd go from here.

"Yes, but one thing first." He pulled me in and kissed me as we stood next to the driver's door of the van. "Want to get something to eat on the way home or should we order something to be delivered?"

"I think I'd like to go out to dinner. I mean as long as there's a place nearby that has burgers and fries," I said and settled my hands on his hips.

"Okay, follow me," he said, and I watched as he walked around the back of the building where I knew he parked his car. I was about to get in the car when I noticed Anna across the street staring at where Cole was. She didn't move a muscle as she continued to stare. Then I noticed her lips were moving, but she was far enough away I had no clue what she was saying. Suddenly she turned and met my eyes.

"*You have not defeated me. Cole will pay with his life for taking what was mine.*" It was her voice, or similar to her voice, but I heard it in my mind rather than my ears.

"You'll never touch Cole," I growled low and menacing, and hoped she heard it.

Her lips lifted in a smile before she turned and walked away just as Cole pulled out of the parking lot and waved to me while he slowly drove down the street. I looked again but Anna was gone. I backed the van out of the parking space and followed Cole, but I couldn't shake the feeling that Anna had a plan, and she wasn't going to give up until one of us was dead and she had the power she so desperately wanted.

Cole stopped at a small local burger place, and I hurried out of the van to meet him at the window. After ordering, we sat at one of the small outdoor tables and waited for our food. I kept expecting Anna to appear somewhere, and I couldn't stop myself from looking around.

"Bobby?"

"Sorry, I missed that," I said and glanced over his shoulder.

"I saw her too, she tried to enter my mind, but I blocked her," Cole said, bringing my full attention to him.

"She spoke to me mentally," I whispered and hoped like hell no one nearby heard me.

"I heard her. I tried to protect you, but I couldn't. She's trying to scare us, and she knows we care about each other so she's trying to use those emotions to distract us from her real plan."

"What's her real plan?" I asked and leaned in close.

"She still wants the power, but Haniel did not choose her or Nox. She knows this but she thinks she can take it." His eyes blinked rapidly as he spoke, and I imagined him watching what he was describing in his mind.

"Cole, she threatened you," I whispered.

"I know, but she doesn't know what's happened yet. She thinks she still has the advantage, but tonight she'll find out how wrong she is." His eyes opened and his expression softened. "Don't worry, when the time comes, you'll know what to do."

I wanted to trust him, but I was still in the dark where he obviously knew way more than me. "I don't want you to get hurt." He covered my hand with his and was about to say something when our order was announced. He smiled and kissed my cheek before standing.

"It's all going to be as it's meant to be," he said before walking up to the pick-up window.

THIRTY-SEVEN

Cole

I TRIED TO GIVE Bobby privacy and not listen to his thoughts, but it was harder when he was so worried and frightened. Anna had accomplished exactly what she wanted it to. She'd put Bobby on alert for anything that could happen to me and taken his focus off her. He kept looking around for her, but she wasn't nearby. She was already at her farm preparing for later.

"Here you go," I said and put his burger and fries in front of him. "She's not here. I'd know if she was. You can relax." His eyes met mine searching for deceit. Since my mind had been expanded, I knew his thoughts, but I forced myself not to act by anything other than his words.

"You really can hear thoughts," Bobby said as though he only in that moment realized it was true.

"Yes, but I'm making myself not hear yours. I want to hear what you think through your words, not your thoughts."

"Thank you for being honest. I know you said you could do it, and I wanted to believe you. But I also hoped it wasn't true because I didn't want you to know everything about me." Bobby was so honest, and I appreciated that more than I would ever be able to show him. But I was willing to put in the time to try. He took one last look around the street before picking up his burger and taking a bite.

"How was your day?" I asked, and for the next hour the two of us forgot we were in some strange new world and just enjoyed each other's company.

"Did you want to go to my house for a while?" I asked, and hoped he would say yes.

He looked at the time and thought about it for a second before answering. "Sure. I can't stay late though. Dad won't be as nice tomorrow." He chuckled. "Let's go before it gets too late." The two of us stood and once again went to our separate cars and he followed me home.

"I'm glad you decided to stay a while," I said when I walked up to where he was just getting out of his car. *Anna is nearby, tonight is when she intends to try to take the power.* He stiffened for a split-second as I took his hand but then he squeezed my fingers. He'd heard me. *Don't be afraid, she can't hear me, and I can protect you. But you won't need it.*

"Me too, I hope we have more orders in this area so I can stop by more often," Bobby said, but I could feel the tension in his thoughts and hear it in his voice.

Once we were inside, I locked the door and put my finger up to my lips. "We'll need to speak quietly. Even though I removed all the symbols we'd drawn and diminished her powers here, she can still hear us if she tries hard enough."

"Cole, are you sure you can do this?"

I took his face in my hands and met his beautiful eyes. "Yes, and after tonight we'll never need to be afraid again." He nodded and glanced around the room.

"Is there something else we should be doing?"

"No, she's nearly here," I said, just as the door blew open sending splinters of wood and debris all over the room.

"I told you this power was meant for me. I won't stand back while you squander it," Anna screamed as she levitated up to the door.

"What is she?" Bobby asked from where he was squatted down with his arms over his head.

"It's not Anna. Not anymore," I said and walked toward her. *I know what you are, but you were not chosen for this power, and you have no say in who wields it. Tonight, your story ends.*

She sneered at me, and I knew she'd heard me, but she still levitated just inside the door. Her long grey hair swirled around her head in a wind born of magic and whatever darkness she used to show me she did indeed have power. I stood and walked closer to her. "Is Anna still in there?" I asked and again she sneered.

"You have no idea what you speak of," she growled.

"You have no idea what I learned last night. Much has happened since we saw you last, the least of which is I now know exactly what you are. Nox was your nephew, but you lied when you said you didn't know where he was. He inhabited this body for a while after he forced Anna's spirit out."

"Cole?" Bobby asked.

"He sacrificed his aunt's spirit to a demon so he could inhabit her body. You see, Nox wasn't born with magical abilities, but Anna was."

"I took what was mine. She didn't want to use it and didn't deserve to be blessed with so much power," Anna screamed.

"But that wasn't the end of it was it, Urkinoth." Her smile widened unnaturally, and her face seemed to melt and form into a completely different shape. Spiney horns grew from both sides of her head and draped over her back revealing her true form. A demon.

"She fought me. A simple human tried to take my power away. The power I was promised. The boy was easy to manipulate, he wanted power nearly as much as I did. But when his spirit was in her body there was enough of her left to fight him, and me." Her nails extended into knife-like claws that she raked along the wall as she moved closer to us.

"Did you really think Haniel would grant you the power you desired? She is, after all, an archangel." I waited for her reaction and put myself between the demon and Bobby. "Why would an archangel give a demon the power of sight, and the ability to hear thoughts?" My voice started to take on the power of the gift and the demon noticed. "You are not worthy." Lightning crackled from my fingertips, and I stepped closer.

"Two sacrifices, that was the cost. The archangel promised me power for two souls," the demon snarled as she grew in size to where she nearly touched the ceiling. "A weak human will not tell me anything," she growled and gnashed her teeth while she floated toward me. "You are nothing but a weak insect who has no power over me." She gripped the front of my shirt and pulled me in close to her as the toes of my shoes barely touched the floor. "Tonight, there will be two more sacrifices to Haniel."

She released me suddenly and I took a step back, and right into Bobby's chest. One look and I knew Haniel was right: he was the guardian, and he was my sword.

THIRTY-EIGHT

Bobby

I WATCHED AS THE old woman I knew as Anna was transformed into a horrible creature. I was so shocked I couldn't do anything but cower on the floor. I listened as Cole stood up to the demon with no fear and put himself in front of me.

The demon threatened him. Threatened us both. And something in me changed. The sting of electricity shot through my veins and a voice boomed in my head. *"You are my sword. You will protect the power and the chosen one."*

I started to stand just as the demon advanced on Cole and he didn't back down. His clenched fists started to crackle with the power of the blue lightning, but the voice in my head was there again even louder. "*You are my sword!*"

Jumping up I could feel the power course through me, and I knew what I needed to do. Cole and I were one, he was the one I was made to protect, and his power would change everything. Throwing my arm out, a sword of lightning and blue flames appeared in my hand.

"Stand back," I yelled at the demon. At first it looked from me to Cole unsure who was the bigger threat, and when Cole was shoved into my chest, that's all it took to put me in motion. I was his protector, and nothing would ever hurt him again. Tucking him behind me, I pointed the sword at the demon.

"You really think you can hurt me with that?" the demon asked and seemed to grow even bigger.

"I know I can." I lunged forward and drove the sword into its chest. It bellowed so loudly the house shook and I was thrown back away from where it struggled to pull the sword from its chest. It shrieked and screamed while clawing at the sword, but its hands only passed through it.

Cole slowly walked around me and touched my arm when he passed by. Everything seemed to slow down, and he turned to look at me and smiled the way he had this morning when we had been in bed together. Full of love, and trust, and everything good in the world. He then turned to the demon and gripped the sword. "I banish you in the name of the archangel Haniel. You will never return to this world again."

His whole body ignited with the blue lightning and a bolt of it shot down the sword into the demon. It screamed before it was blown apart and drifted away on small glowing bits of ash that disappeared before they drifted to the floor. He spun around to me just as the sword appeared again in my hand, still flaming a brilliant blue.

"You're beautiful," he said before rushing into my arms. "My sword."

I wasn't sure exactly what that meant, but I knew no matter what it was I'd be there for him whenever he needed me, and we would figure out exactly what our roles were. "Are you okay?" I asked him and held him at arm's length to get a good look.

"I'm fine. There was nothing it could have done that would have hurt me. But I wouldn't have been able to destroy it without you. I can hold the sword but only you can use it when needed. I didn't understand what Haniel meant when she said you would be my guardian and my sword, but now I know." Cole looked at me like he was seeing me for the first time, and I understood exactly how he felt. He was fire and electricity all in one. And his power was amazing, but he needed protection. I would be his sword and I would strike down anything that tried to hurt him.

"I will always be there for you," I said, and I meant it with every cell in my body. "I will be your sword." His hand glowed a pale blue as he reached for me.

"And I will be your heart, together nothing can stop us, and soon the other demons and creatures of the night that try to take powers meant for good will know." Cole met my eyes again before pressing his lips against mine. "Thank you. You could have chosen to walk away that day when you saw me hit with the bolt from the blue."

"Nothing would have made me leave you. I needed to know you were okay." It was true and the strange pull to him made more sense. We'd both been chosen that day, but we both had to choose to accept our destiny.

"You really are my guardian," Cole said, and held me close. I wasn't sure how all this would work, but we'd figure it out. And if anyone or anything was stupid enough to think they could hurt him, they'd have to go through me first, and my sword. My super cool demon killing, flaming sword. Cole pulled back and met my eyes.

"Really?" he said with a smirk.

"You promised you wouldn't read my mind all the time," I reminded him.

"You were screaming it so it made it a little hard to ignore. I was imagining you spiking a ball into the ground and doing a victory dance. Whatever that looks like," Cole said. It was obvious he didn't feel guilty at all.

I breathed out a deep sigh and crossed my arms. "So, this is my life now."

Cole ruffed up my hair and kissed me with a smack. "No, this is our life."

EPILOGUE

Three Years Later

Cole

TIME MOVED ON, SOME things changed, while a lot stayed the same. I still worked at Brian's Sporting Goods, and Bobby still worked at the copy shop. But mostly we did it because both of us really liked our jobs and these days it was a nice break from when we'd be on an assignment that typically involved a demon.

We lived together in our own house now. It was a bit remote but was right in the middle between Hickory Crossing and Sugarfield so our families could visit if they wanted to, and we both had an easy drive to work.

"You're sure it's the same carnival?" I asked as both of us hurried to get dressed.

"Yes, I drove by it on the way home yesterday. I recognized the big tent. It's the same."

"Do you think it's a good idea to go back?" Three years ago, when I was still trying to figure out what was happening to me, going to that carnival had lifted the veil for me on what my abilities could be. It was terrifying, but it was also amazing, and once I was able to control the constant thoughts of other people and press them down into the background, it was all okay.

"Yes. I want to actually go to the carnival this time. They have a lot of different acts, and activities. I mean it's not every day the carnival comes to town," Bobby said with a grin and a kiss to my cheek.

"Then I guess we're going to the carnival," I said.

We drove along the freeway until the big tent and Ferris wheel came into view. The sun was just setting as we excited the freeway and drove along the small country road that led to the empty field where we'd parked last time. "It's nice to get to drive together this time," Bobby said.

"It is, and it's been nice to have a little break from hunting." I looked at the entrance and all the people walking toward it while we drove around looking for an open parking space.

"Is that what we do? I thought it was more like searching," he said.

"Hunting, searching, either way it always ends the same. One more demon sent to where they can never come back."

"One less is always good," Bobby said as he pulled into a parking space. I'd accepted my ability to read thoughts and interpret visions that helped us find other demons who tried to hide among us, but when he accepted the task of being my sword, I knew together we'd be unstoppable. And so far, we were.

"I finally told Mom about Anna," I said. He knew I was going to. We'd talked about it, and I didn't want to keep lying to my parents. His family already knew and while his dad only wanted to know what was absolutely necessary, his mom worked with us regularly. She and her friends, who all possessed different talents, worked to keep the balance between dark and light on the side of light.

"What did she say?" Bobby asked.

"At first, she didn't believe me. But then she said she'd noticed Anna had changed. She'd gone from being friendly but aloof to someone who rarely interacted with anyone in town. She said it made her sad to know she was killed because of her nephew."

"I'm sorry, baby, I know you hoped it would turn out differently than it did." Bobby turned in the seat to face me before reaching for my hand.

"Yes, I did. But we can't change what fate has mapped out for us. We can only follow the signs and hope for the best." There were so many things I'd been shown. Some were wonderful and I looked forward to them, and the life I knew I'd share with Bobby. But some were horrible. And most of those I tried to keep to myself. "Ready to go inside?"

Bobby nodded before we got out of the car and he held my hand while we walked across the dusty parking lot to the entrance. The same two men were working at the entrance; one of them walked over to us wearing a warm smile.

"Good evening, gentlemen. I see you've returned," he said with a tip of his hat.

"I remember you," Bobby said. "Thank you for your help."

"I don't believe I helped you at all," he said and handed each of us a ticket for entry.

"How much do we owe you?" I asked.

"Complimentary. Go and enjoy the show," the other man said.

"Thank you so much," Bobby said, and took them from him. "Come on, Cole, let's go watch the Flying Galliers." He pulled me along, down a row of carnival games that led to the big tent in the middle.

"The what?" I asked having no clue what he was talking about.

"Acrobats, they're supposed to be really good, and their show is about to start."

I laughed as he pulled me through the crowd that grew thicker the closer we got to the big red and white tent, but then off by itself just past the midway, I noticed another much smaller tent. A large sign promised palm reading and fortune telling. The flaps of the tent were open, but the interior was dark enough I couldn't tell what it looked like inside. Next to the entrance stood a woman with long dark hair, leaning against the ropes that held up the tent.

Her eyes met mine, and even at this distance I knew she was not just an act. She was the real thing. Power emanated from her, and I forced myself not to even try to read her thoughts. I knew I wouldn't be able to.

"Cole, did you want something to eat before we go in?" Bobby asked, drawing my attention to him.

"Sure, I could eat," I said and looked back at the tent. The woman who'd been there was gone, but I could still feel her power.

"Let's hurry, I don't want to be late." Bobby led us to the nearest food vendor where we both chose a hotdog and a drink before hurrying to the entrance of the tent. I thought back to three years ago and how this carnival had opened my eyes, and my thoughts.

"Do you think we'd have known that Anna was blocking my powers if we hadn't come here?" I asked Bobby, who was busy eating his hotdog.

"Well, I'd like to think we would have figured it out eventually. But I'm not sure." I followed him up an aisle until we found two open seats and sat down.

"Me either. But I'm happy you figured it out. You were my sword and my guardian all along." He grinned at me around a mouthful of food before leaning in and kissing my cheek.

"Always. There's nothing I won't do for you," he said, and I knew he meant every word.

THE END

CARNIVAL OF MYSTERIES 2

ONCE MORE WE BID you Welcome, Travelers, toErrante Ame's Carnival of Mysteries! Join us for another round of fantastic,space-and-time spanning tales by a talented group of some of the best authorsto be found in M/M romance. Whether you enjoy mystery, action, danger, or justsweet romance, there is something for everyone at the Carnival!

Rook'sTime -- Kim Fielding

TheWrong Familiar -- Megan Derr

TheVillain Who Wasn't -- Liv Rancourt

BlueLightning -- BL Maxwell

MagicEscaping -- Kaje Harper

Lightin the Darkness -- Eden Winters

You CanSave Me -- RL Merrill

Go forthe Climate -- Ander C. Lark

Flamesof the Arcane -- Nicole Dennis

AirsAbove the Ground -- Rachel Langella

Midnighton the Midway -- Morgan Brice

DustBowl Magic -- Zam Maxfield

Dragonspark-- Elizabeth Silver

About the Author

BL Maxwell grew up in a small town listening to her grandfather spin tales about his childhood. Later she became an avid reader and after a certain vampire series she became obsessed with fanfiction. She soon discovered Slash fanfiction and later discovered the MM genre and was hooked.

Many years later, she decided to take the plunge and write down some of the stories that seem to run through her head late at night when she's trying to sleep.

BL Maxwell loves to hear from readers who enjoy her stories, so feel free to reach out at any of these links:

Amazon: https://www.amazon.com/stores/BL-Maxwell/author/B07CZQ1RN7

Website: https://blmaxwellwriter.com/ (Free book)

Newsletter: https://sendfox.com/blmaxwell

Facebook: https://www.facebook.com/bl.maxwell.35/

Bookbub: https://www.bookbub.com/profile/bl-maxwell

BingeBooks: https://bingebooks.com/profile/blmaxwell

Also By BL Maxwell

Thank you for reading Blue Lightning

Dead But Not Gone-Spirit Boys Book Three Coming September 2024

Series Link: https://www.amazon.com/dp/B0CR-PZKRQ

Enjoy a FREE copy of A Night To Remember . A short story with Andy and Link.

https://books2read.com/u/baDrw8

Enjoy a FREE copy of The Cemetery Tour a Valley Ghosts Short Story.

https://books2read.com/CemeteryTour

It was just a fun Halloween activity until the ghosts showed up.

Jason Thomas has always loved the supernatural, and anything to do with ghosts. But when it comes to going on haunted tours he'd rather not. His boyfriend Wade books a tour for them at the local cemetery before Halloween thinking it would be fun way to get in the mood for the holiday.

Being connected to the other side of the veil, it doesn't take long for Wade to start noticing a few strange happenings. When ghosts from the past show themselves followed by other paranormal events, they both know there is more going on than a haunted cemetery tour.

This is a Valley Ghosts short story and also foretells events that happen in The Things We Lose. #MM Paranormal Romance, #FREE reads, #Ghost Story

Below Deck

https://books2read.com/BelowDeck

JJ Carrington was born with a silver spoon in his mouth. He's used to flying in business class and spending all his holidays at the nicest resorts in the world. But lately he's tired of the same vacation over and over again, and the one-night stands that seem to plague him.

Cory Wynn has been working on a cruise ship for the past year. He'd never traveled before that, and now he's seen more of the Caribbean than he even knew existed. He hoped to meet someone to fall in love with while at sea, but so far all he does is work.

When JJ ends up partying late into the night with some of the passengers from a cruise ship, he follows them onboard. But when Cory finds him sleeping in a deckchair after the ship has sailed, he takes him to his cabin. JJ is used to getting his way in everything in life, but he may have met his match in the cruise worker who can't wait until the next stop to get him off the ship. #oppositesattract #smalltown/city #vacationromance

Divided

https://books2read.com/BLDivided

The four Stroud brothers were all born into magic, and when they all come of age their powers will be revealed. It all sounds like a fairytale, but not all magic is good. Their mother embraced the darkness and paid with her life.

Finn Stroud was happy working on the family farm until the day his father announced it was time for them all to go out and find their place in the world, and their magic. He and his four brothers knew this was the tradition of the Imagi people who were meant to wield elemental magic, but Finn soon finds how ill prepared he was for the real world.

Alwin travels from town to town using his own brand of magic to get what he can from anyone that crosses his path. His luck runs out and he's left along the side of the road in a rainstorm. Finn offers him shelter and Alwin offers to guide him in the ways of magic, but everything has a price.

A dark fairytale retelling of The Four Clever Brothers.

#mmromance #mmfairytaleromance #mmfairytaleretelling #magicalrealism #gayromance #darkfairytale #darkromance

Faded Dreams

Blinding Light Book Two

https://books2read.com/FadedDreams

Blinding Light: https://books2read.com/BlindingLight

Rory Smith has been playing bass for Blinding Light since the beginning. Sure, he left a few times temporarily, but he's always gone back to the only life he's really known. It was all fun and games in his twenties, but lately he wonders if there's something more out there besides traveling show to show.

Kai Marshall has always been a huge fan of Blinding Light, but the real reason he goes to every show he can sneak into is to get a glimpse of their hot bass player. Everyone else worshiped the lead singer Easy Rian. When they found out, he was out and proud, and in a relationship with the new guitar player, many hearts were broken. But not his. His heart only beats for Rory, the white-blonde haired rock god that he can't get out of his head.

Rory's played the rockstar game for many years. Not one time in all those years has he met anyone who made him feel the way the cute guy off to the side with the haunting blue eyes does. He's always kept his heart of lockdown, but maybe it's time for a jailbreak. His dreams have faded, but they're not completely gone. #agegap #oppositesattract #friendstolovers #rockstarromance https://books2read.com/ColdBlood

Cold Blood Warm Heart

A Consortium Trilogy Short Story

Leon is adjusting to his new existence as a vampire, but so far Ben has kept him safely isolated in the wilderness of Alaska where he was created.

It's past time for Leon to prove he can control his urges and Ben thinks he has the perfect solution. He wants Leon to spend time with his friends Brennan and Lucas, and hopes his new mate is ready to be out in the world of humans. Ben and Leon are newly mated vampires trying to find their place in the world. Somehow spending Christmas with two more vampires is the least shocking thing in this new world Leon is trying to navigate.

#ParanormalRomance, #MMParanormal, #FatedMates, #Vampires

BETTER TOGETHER Series

Better Together

Chains Required

The First Twelve

The Better Together Boxset

VALLEY GHOSTS Series

Ghost Hunted

Ghost Haunted

Ghost Trapped

Ghost Hexed

Ghost Handled

Ghost Shadow

Haunting Destiny

THE STONE Series

Stone Under Skin

Blood Beneath Stone

Stone Hearts

The Stone Series Box Set

SMALL TOWN CITY series

Remember When

A Night to Remember (Short Story)

Try To Forget

Try To Remember (Short Story)

One Last Chance

Remember Always (Coming Soon)

CONSORTIUM TRILOGY

Burning Addiction

Freezing Aversion

Cold Blood Warm Heart (Short Story)

Melting Darkness

FOUR PACKS Trilogy

The Slow Death

The Ultimate Sacrifice

The Final Salvation

BLINDING LIGHT Series

Blinding Light

Faded Dreams

Just The Right Chord (Short Story)

PM KISSES

Peppermint Mocha Kisses

Sugar and Spice Kisses

Lobster Tales Duology

Green Eyed Boy

Brown Eyed Boy

Spirit Boys Series

Just Another Day At The Morgue (Prequel)

Dead Things

Living With The Dead

Book three Coming September 2024)

STANDALONE

The List

Double Black Diamonds

Ride: The Chance of a Lifetime

Check Yes or No

A Ghost of a Chance

Tutu

Salt & Lime

Amos Ridge

Six Months

Ten or Fifteen Miles

The Snake in the Castle

A Beach Far Away

Just Another Day At The Morgue

A Lot of Snow For Christmas

Divided

Below Deck

COLLECTIONS

Spirits, Teeth and Wings (A Taste of Paranormal Romance)

The Stone Series Boxset

Four Packs Trilogy Collection

Better Together Universe Boxset

Valley Ghosts Boxset 1

Valley Ghosts Boxset 2